A Thousand Tiny Cracks

Stella Maddox

ALL THINGS

THAT MATTER
PRESS

A Thousand Tiny Cracks
Copyright © 2013 by Stella Maddox

ISBN: 978-0-9885427-8-5

Library of Congress Control Number: 2013933401

Cover Design by All Things That Matter Press

Published in 2013 by All Things That Matter Press

For my husband.
No matter where we go from here, we go together.

***

I'll be your dream,
I'll be your wish, I'll be your fantasy
I'll be your hope, I'll be your love
Be everything that you need
I love you more with every breath
Truly, madly, deeply do
-Savage Garden

***

Acknowledgments

I owe huge thanks to:

~Deb and Phil Harris for taking a chance on me.

~Joanna, who told me to unleash my frustration and write it down.

~Sherre, who read my first awful revision and encouraged me anyway.

~Debbie, who spent more time analyzing this text than anyone should.

~Matt, who put aside his own writing to help mold mine. The story is a thousand times better because of you.

~Brittany, who helped me separate illusion from reality.

~Joe, who made me laugh when I wanted to cry.

~Mike, who helped me decide which scenes to fight for.

~Cate, who sat through numerous lunches and feigned interest.

~Whit, for my gorgeous author picture.

~Jennifer and Amy, who both helped me select an excerpt and critiqued my trailer.

~Hungry Lucy, for the use of A Lifetime Remains in my video trailer and their other songs that loop on my iPod as I write.

~My mom, for being patient enough to not read the book until it's released without making me feel guilty. I can stand anyone's criticism but yours.

PART I

2006

Chapter 1 ~ January

Ethan taps me on the shoulder as I perch on the brink of sleep after settling baby Zach into bed for the second time tonight. "You awake?" Air pushes out of my chest the moment the words leave his lips and I consider my answer.

Discussions at bedtime agitate Ethan. His mind spins as he reviews the day and fixates on his unresolved problems, so no conversations of importance begin at this time of night. But if I answer "No" the lie is obvious and he'll roll over in a huff and go to sleep. This is our evening routine: I feel pressure, he feels rejection. Story of our lives.

"Yes, I'm awake." His index finger silently traces a line up my arm before moving toward its destination. "I'm really tired, Ethan. Can we skip this part tonight?"

Ethan pauses. "Are you sure? We don't have to." But we do. It's easier to roll over and do it to avoid the fight.

"It's okay," I respond, trying to convince myself as well. "You know I'll wake up once we get started."

Ethan's hips raise as he slithers out of his pajama pants. He rolls to me and peels off my fuzzy sweatpants and tank top with skill resulting from years of practice. As he climbs above me, I appreciate his athletic body, sculpted from hours of training for races and lifting weights.

His lips gently bump mine as he pushes through familiar territory. Our bodies command us through a well-rehearsed silent performance with no conscious director. Ethan nibbles down the side of my neck and breathes heavily in my ear. As he builds to a slow, steady rhythm, he shifts his weight onto a pillow beside me, seeking a more comfortable position, no longer parallel with me.

My eyes open, searching for him in the soft glow of the alarm clock. His breath puffs in time with his body, as if he is running on the treadmill, and small beads of sweat appear on his brow. Ethan's eyes are closed as he concentrates intently on our pleasure.

"Hey." I bump his nose with mine.

"Hey," he responds. His eyes open and meet mine momentarily before traveling down to appraise my breasts. He catches himself and his eyes return to mine, but the damage is done. My connection is lost.

"It's okay. You can watch."

Ethan gives me a naughty smile, appreciating my acceptance. He pulls back to the side a bit further to increase his field of vision, but my eyes remain focused on his the entire time.

"You can relax, you know," Ethan whispers. "I'm right here."

I close my eyes, attempting to surrender. The heat pump repairman will be here in the morning. I scheduled the appointment early so that I can make it to my strength class at the gym on time. Oh, and I meant to mention the smell in the laundry room to Ethan.

All of my chores line themselves up in my mind. I chase them away, but somehow they return to torment me every time the clock circles. I want to discuss them with Ethan, to process the never-ending list so maybe I can disengage from it. But he isn't here right now, whether he claims to be or not. He doesn't comprehend that his own actions destroy this intimacy that he physically pushes on me constantly.

Refocus. My eyes open to the sight of his furry chest and the trail of hair that leads down to the point where we merge, forcing me into the present. I pursue my pleasure, forgoing the bond with Ethan. The pace increases from rhythmic to frantic and my body slips into the familiar routine. We climax together, each completely focused on only ourselves.

***

"Shush." I hear a giggle across the bed and feel the covers shift.

"Mommy's sleeping. Don't wake her up." Giggle. Shush. Giggle. Shush.

I lay in my own little tomb under the sheet, listening and trying not to move. Maybe, if I don't breathe, they will leave me alone. Maybe they will drag Ethan downstairs and leave me in my bliss. Well, almost bliss. I do need to pee rather badly. Crap. Now I thought about it. Ugh, maybe if I barely move my leg I won't notice it. Oh, that only made it worse. Shit. I fly out of bed to the bathroom. The giggles cease; Mommy is awake.

We trudge down the steps to start our day while the pipes upstairs spring to life, indicating Ethan is drawing a hot bath to ease his way into morning.

And it begins.

"Can I eat spaghetti for breakfast?" Maya, whose unpredictable food choices at age four disrupt every meal, wants to know.

"No. There is no pasta," I reply.

"Pop-Tart, Pop-Tart, Pop-Tart," chants Zach, who at two has spent his entire life existing on Pop Tarts. When Maya was young, I assuaged my guilt about working by preparing a variety of delicious, homemade baby foods. Poor Zach is lucky if I remember to feed him. Pop-Tart and cracker are his two favorite words. I stick a Pop-Tart in his mouth and toss him into the high chair.

The refrigerator slams shut. "There's nothing to eat," Maya whines.

I begin my waiter impersonation. "Well, today, madam, we offer a wide array of breakfasts. We have frozen waffles, cinnamon raisin bagels, Cheerios, or fresh fruit."

"Yuck," she replies.

The phone chirps. Crap. I forgot that the furnace guy is scheduled to arrive in the next thirty minutes. Sure enough, he leaves a message on the machine confirming the appointment. Thank God. That heat pump hasn't worked right for two months and it's freaking cold in here.

But back to the issue at hand.

"What would you like to eat?"

"What are you having?"

"An egg."

"I don't like eggs."

And we go on and on, until I finally pop a piece of toast on a plate, smother it in jelly, and place it in front of her chair, an offering to an erratic god.

Ethan scoots by us, grabs a protein bar, and pecks me on the cheek as he unplugs his phone from the charger. "Don't forget I have that management training class today." He slides the phone into his pocket and clips his hospital ID tag to his scrubs as he reviews his schedule. "And I'm supposed to meet Mark at the gym this evening, so I'll probably be home around seven." His days expand until he is absent almost every hour that our children are awake. Does he consciously plan to avoid us? Have I ever seen him hurry or modify his schedule if I ask him for something? He flies out the door.

Time to get dressed. I check the clock. Seven forty-three a.m. Just enough time to throw on some clothes, consult with the heater guy, and drag the kids to the gym. While they eat, I launch myself up the stairs, select a work-out outfit, and yank my hair into a lumpy ponytail while examining the crow's feet that trench their way around my eyes. I'm thirty-one. When did I start to feel so old? I pinch my cheeks and hope that suffices as makeup as I run back down.

Meanwhile, Zach has grabbed the jellied toast from Maya, shredded it to tiny pieces, and dropped it like a starburst in a giant circle around his high chair. His ears, his nose, and, I swear, each individual strand of his hair are all smothered in jelly. Maya trickles up the steps to capture a cat that lurks in the corner as it tries to break free and sprint to the litter box. Is it really possible that they did all this in less than fourteen seconds?

I wash the jelly off of Zach, set him on the kitchen floor, and begin to clean. "Aye," he yells, and toddles off after the cat.

After scrubbing the floor, I retrieve Zach, drag him up the steps, pin him down, and attempt to wrestle clothes onto him. Dressing a rabid squirrel would be less challenging. Maya emerges from her room wearing a monstrous pink ensemble. Her hot pink pants, baby pink skirt, bright pink character tee, and array of bracelets and necklaces clash, and not in a funky well-dressed kind of way. "Beautiful," I say, and aim her toward her shoes.

The door is close. I see the escape. The sun reflects off the windshield in the driveway. If we proceed a little farther and make it to the minivan, the kids can play in it while I deal with the furnace guy. Then I will drive to the gym, where my freedom awaits. Once I pack the kids away in the childcare, the blaring music and the misery of squats and lunges will dull my mind. We almost make it. Our coats are on, and then I hear it. "But Mommy, I didn't eat anything." I sink down beside the door and start to cry.

Where is Ethan when I need him? I wish I could mummify myself and return to bed. Ethan occupied me for half the night, so my four hours of sleep aren't reinforcing my patience. The evening did, however, put enough spring in his step to thwart an attack from the kids and bounce him out the door after his luxurious private bath.

An image of his private college dorm room flashes into my head: a loft separating the room into two spaces vertically since it was too small to do anything but. Ethan clasped my hands, intertwining our fingers and our souls as we combined our bodies and our lives. The mirror above us, shocking to me simply in its presumption of existing, reflected his passion and allowed me to observe every movement's external counterpoint as I felt it from within. His eyes, never leaving mine, twinkled in the Christmas lights that he strung for ambiance and left hanging through the year. Some of the most important nights of my life were spent huddled under that loft, bobbling softly up and down in Ethan's illegal water-bed, his strong arms stabilizing me.

The phone blares with Ethan's familiar ringtone. It must be important. We rarely communicate since he is busy learning his new routine at work. And it isn't like he wants to hear it anyway. He still exists in the outside world and has conversations and deadlines and goals that have nothing to do with diapers or food. He eats lunch every day with no one hanging on him, no one screaming at him, no one expecting him to jump up fifteen times during his meal for milk or thrown food.

"Hey," I answer, "I was just thinking about you. What's up?"

Before he can reply, a screech reverberates from the basement. Shit. The kids wandered off and I didn't even notice.

I scurry down the steps while Ethan announces, "My oil light came on this morning." That's it. No request. No petition for help or hesitation in the demand. His next sentence is garbled as I pull both Zach and Maya, protesting, off of the giant plastic Flintstone-feet car that resides in the basement and set them each in an isolated chair. I yank their coats off, point to emphasize the seriousness of the offense, and snarl to indicate that they are in time out.

The phone line is silent. "What was that? Sorry. Maya trapped Zach in the back of that Flintstone car and wouldn't let him out."

Ethan sighs, indicating the end of the conversation. "I have to work, Stella. Just add the oil to your list."

"Done," I say. Ethan hangs up. Wonderful. Now both vehicles need oil changes, not to mention I still need to replace the brakes on my van. He drives by no less than five service locations every day and could easily drop off a car and ride with a co-worker to the office. I took responsibility for all of those duties when I worked. But, hell, no. I have to call to schedule the damn appointment and co-ordinate his ride in to work, even though I barely know anyone in this Appalachian, southern Tennessee hell that someone named Greeneville. We've only lived here six months. So instead, I'll drag the kids over, along with all the necessary food, toys, and clothing, and sit for two hours in the waiting room. It will waste my entire afternoon.

As I return my phone to my gym bag, I smell the laundry room. The fucking cat litter. I want to offload the cats. Ethan disagrees. He volunteered to be the cat litter pooper scooper. During my pregnancies, when I was not allowed to touch it, the job fell to him. When we made the decision to keep the cats, I was quite clear that I would only agree to it if he took care of them. For some reason, though, Ethan seems immune to cat pee stink. It builds and builds and he ignores it, as if it might clean itself up while his eye is turned. I guess this is his lucky day.

The litter box resides in the laundry room. I hate it with a passion only second to the passion with which I resent my husband. Between fourteen loads of laundry per week, with a three-hour dry time per load thanks to the crap dryer that we need to replace, I spend a good amount of time in this tiny stinky room. Every time I pass through, grainy litter tracks scatter. Not to mention it sticks to the clean wet clothes if they happen to fall on the floor. I can't take it anymore. Last week the cats started peeing in the kids' toy room because their litter box was so nasty that even they wouldn't use it.

"Can we get down?" Maya calls. I can't even think about shit without interruption.

I peer into the basement. Maya and Zach still perch on their chairs in the same positions as when I left them. Everything in me wants to scream, "No. Just sit there forever," but I don't. Instead, I say, "Can I turn on a cartoon for you guys?"

The kids snuggle in for a show and I take control of the stinky litter. I clean the box, which probably hasn't been done in six weeks, and Lysol the entire area. I have no idea why we bag Zach's dirty stinky diapers and dispose of them outside but keep fifteen pounds of cat shit right outside the den. I scrub their food bowls and decide it is time to insist on a bagging-the-poop policy. I worry Ethan will discern my level of frustration and decide that if he procrastinates enough, I'll just clean it without complaint.

A neighbor from across the street dropped by to introduce herself a few days ago and I issued an invitation for a play date for our daughters. But now the kids can't even play where the toys are because it reeks so horribly and I'm embarrassed. Ethan doesn't notice because he doesn't spend all day in this house smelling it. He walks out the door and pretends like it doesn't exist. Of course, that's his specialty.

I wish I could call Ethan. I just talked to him, but I still feel totally and utterly alone, although I'm constantly surrounded by chaos and noise.

Since I left my engineering career to stay home, he has completely forgotten about everything that happens here. We used to share the dishes, the cooking, the laundry, and the cleaning. But now, he rules the roost. He doesn't manage these monsters, help with the dishes, or even pretend to give a shit about grocery shopping or cooking. I could tolerate it if he didn't just totally ignore it, like what I do doesn't even matter. I spend most of my time feeling like a ghost. No one actually talks to me or asks me how I am or how my day went. I'm just the ghost in the background who keeps everyone else's life going.

My entire life is defined as Maya's mom or Ethan's wife. Yesterday, Maya spilled juice on her shirt and Ethan said, "Don't worry. Just put it downstairs. It'll get washed." I almost blew. As if he ever notices that there's laundry to do. Apparently, his clothes magically clean themselves and sprint back up the stairs to jump into his closet.

I am tired of being ignored. I tell myself that raising our children and caring for our home is a worthwhile job—and I try like hell to believe it. The problem is that this job has no rewards. No one ever says, "Great job Mom, you cleaned up another meal," or, "Nice catch," when a Pop-Tart whizzes by my ear. There is not one bit of positive reinforcement during my day.

So, yes, I resent him. I hate him because he is the only one who could give me that reinforcement, but he doesn't. Instead he slinks around the house, hoping I won't assign him any work. He runs to the gym, to play poker, to do anything he can to hide away from here. And the really sad part is that at this point, I dread the nights he is home because we don't talk anyway. He just sits in front of the television and ignores me. Those are the nights I feel the emptiest. Those are the nights I just want to disappear. Our marriage didn't shatter in one day or one argument. It dissolved slowly in the silence while we were too distracted to notice.

He doesn't ask about my day because he doesn't want to hear it. He doesn't want the frustration, doesn't give a shit that the brakes on the van squeak, and wouldn't notice if the heat pump totally froze over except for the fact that his dinner might be cold. But, honestly, I don't think he'd even notice that. What the fuck do I have to do to get his attention?

A knock at the door jolts me out of my thoughts. I flip off the television and herd Maya and Zach, transporting the bag of cat crap and gathering the kids' coats along the way. I open the door to see man who has to be a hundred and four. He smiles and says, "Stella Maddox, right? I hear you need some help with your furnace."

"Absolutely," I tell him. "The heat pump freezes over and refuses to defrost. Our electric bill shot through the roof last month." I trek out the door to examine the furnace, Zach in hand, Maya sniveling along behind us, complaining that she never ate breakfast.

Chapter 2 ~ July

We relax by our backyard pool on sweltering afternoons and enjoy the sunshine. Maya just turned five and is learning to swim. She paddles around in her tiny blue flowered swimsuit, wearing her floppy Hanna Andersson sun hat, and screeching "Look at me" with joy every time her feet leave the bottom of the pool and she doggie paddles a few feet.

Zach will be three next week and finally doesn't have to be carried at all times. He can sit on the deck with a pile of Goldfish crackers or play on the pool steps without being on me. He resembles a tiny suicide bomber in his floaty swimsuit with ballasts all around his pudgy middle. He sits on the top step and dumps his bucket of toys over and over into the pool.

Ethan and I purchased this house not quite a year ago. The pool was the biggest selling point. I swear, we walked in the front door, straight through the kitchen, and a giant beam of light revealed the pool in the backyard. We knew right then that this was the house we would live in.

The realtor said lots of people didn't want the maintenance of the pool, but, for me, it was perfect. Since I am—or was—a biomedical engineer, the giant vat of chemicals in the backyard provides hours of entertainment. We installed all the safety gear. Locks on every door require a key that the kids can't reach. Extra gates prevent access to the pool in case a child manages to escape. We enforce a strict no-child-out-the-door-without-a-parent rule. Most people with pools love to entertain. We generally hate it. Our friends allow their kids to run around the pool with almost no supervision, and the liability terrifies me. I can't lifeguard effectively while engaged in conversation.

"Anyone home?" A voice calls and the top of a head bobbles over the fence.

"Yep. The gate is open, come on through." I only know one person taller than our privacy fence, and I recognize the voice immediately. It's Tad Newlan from next door. All of their names begin with the same letter and it frustrates me trying to remember which name belongs with which guy. His mom, Tracey, was the only one whose name I was sure of for the first six weeks after we moved in.

I say kid, but he's a teenager, a senior in high school if I remember correctly. He's a twin, but not identical. Actually, he and his brother aren't even similar. I can't imagine raising twins. Two kids with space between is miserable enough.

Tad is the oldest by two minutes, a fact he emphasizes at every opportunity. He assisted the previous owner of our house with maintenance, so he knows how to fix almost anything we can't. The older brother syndrome is obvious: he is extremely responsible, overly helpful, and very serious. I don't know many high school boys, but he's interesting to be around. He's intelligent, even if he does seem lost in his own little world at times.

Theo, his twin, is the wild one with his spiky blond hair and eyebrow piercing. His antics entertain us since our bedroom window faces their driveway. Invariably he sets off their dog alarm, two giant Dobermans, in the middle of the night on weekends as he attempts to sneak into the house. He enthusiastically cuts down trees for us and handles all of our large outside problems. He has more initiative than sense, in my opinion, formed as I watched him chase a groundhog across my backyard with a shotgun. I get the impression he only works so he can afford to party.

Both boys occasionally catch us in our driveway to talk. Once either of them starts discussing a topic that they enjoy, it's downright impossible to escape. We call it being "Newlaned," as in, "Damn it, you knew I was in a hurry to meet Dave. Why didn't you interrupt me with a fake phone call or something? You knew I got Newlaned in the driveway. I saw you snickering at the window."

Tad walks through the gate and around the pool, wearing basketball shorts, a sweaty T-shirt, and a goofy pair of sunglasses that obviously rule him out of the popular crowd in high school. Sheesh, that kid needs a makeover or he'll never get laid.

"Want your lawn mowed?" Tad mows our lawn because I want to avoid buying a tractor. We own a push mower, but our acre of property sits on a steep incline, and Ethan would rather expend his energy at the gym than drag a mower around the yard productively. He wants to buy a riding mower, but I stall him because I know he'll just drive around in circles, with his iPod on and the blade off, to escape from the house and stick me with the kids. Or, at least, that's what I'd do. But I can't cut the grass; I'm allergic to it.

"Can you wait a while? The kids are still playing nicely, which happens only when the stars perfectly align. If you start now, I'll have to take them in the house so that I don't swell up like a balloon."

"'Kay," he says. "Do you mind if I jump in your pool to cool off, then?" Tad and his brother had free access to our pool before we arrived. I can't decide if I'm comfortable with that or not. I want to be the cool neighbor. I don't feel like I'm actually that much older than this kid. Not to mention it's nice to have someone around whom I can beckon to help me at a moment's notice, because Ethan isn't too strong in that area.

So Tad pops into the pool. Maya swims right up to him and spins in circles, singing, "I'm a mermaid. Watch me spin!"

The look he gives her says, "Oh, shit," and he ducks under the water and glides to the deep end.

"So what have you been up to lately?" I ask.

"We went camping last week," Tad responds, treading water. "It was miserable. Nothing like being stuck in a tent with your family and no way to escape. I spent most of the time outside by myself."

"I've never camped. I'm a Hilton girl all the way. If there isn't room service and an indoor pool, count me out. Sitting alone outside in the bugs and heat sounds awful."

"At least I could see the stars," he says. "My grandparents purchased a large reflector telescope for the trip, so I spent a lot of time gazing through it. I found a few nebula and I think I managed to spot Andromeda, along with identifying most of the visible constellations. Then my cousin and I disagreed over which star is closest to the earth. What do you think? How do you define a star?"

Maya jumps into the conversation, literally, splashing between us with her pink fishy kickboard. "A star is a giant ball of gas," she shouts. "We learned that in preschool. Do you need to go to preschool?"

"Maya." I glare at her, annoyed, "Yes, a star is a giant ball of gas. Now calm down and don't interrupt adults when they are speaking." I turn to Tad. "But she is right, I'll give her that. So obviously the sun is the closest star to Earth."

"Well, that was the disagreement. I think it's Proxima Centauri."

"Then you'd be wrong," I retort, but smile so he knows I'm teasing. "Perhaps you need to reevaluate your definition."

"But you can't count the sun," he argues, completely serious.

"If you can't include the sun, then you eliminate the other stars as well. By ignoring it, you exclude the others by definition. The only fair way to exclude the sun would be to specify a certain color of star, say only red or yellow. Even if you specify a category, they're both dwarfs, so size isn't enough criteria to distinguish them. If you ask for simply the closest star, you're wrong," I challenge him.

"Do-pin, do-pin," Zach wails as a dolphin that escaped his bucket makes its way through the opening and down the strainer. I go over to save it. About the time I'm bent upside down, peering down the strainer and trying to figure out how to retrieve the dolphin out of a pile of dead bees that I forgot to dump earlier, I realize that Tad is holding on to the pool ladder, watching me. I am conscious of the fact that my blue bikini is starting to ride up in back, but I'm too self-conscious to reach back and pull it down. For a moment, I am hyper-aware of his presence. And while I'm pretty sure I look hot—hopefully he isn't staring in disgust—I'm a married woman, barely clothed, bent over in front of a teenage boy. Somehow this is not feeling appropriate.

The moment passes as Zach slides off the step he has been jumping on, flips under the water, and comes up screaming. Those ballasts on his suit could float a tank, but I dive in and grab him anyway. Maya starts whining immediately as well, just to keep her brother company.

"The alignment has obviously passed," I quip. "Swim as long as you like and feel free to cut the grass whenever."

I gather the kids, pack up our towels and toys, and climb the steps to our house. As I wrangle Zach and Maya through the door, I glance back one more time. This kid interests me. Talking with him resembles any other adult conversation I might have had before I consigned my life to an indentured servitude of diapers and sippy cups. His opinions challenge me to think, even if he is wrong. Our conversation evolved without the common ground that most of my friendships are based on: children sharing activities or husbands who work together.

As I look back, Tad is frozen in the same position, staring at me.

PART II

2007

Ethan opens the door with a smile on his face and strolls into the kitchen.

Perfect, I think, in response to his never-asked question. My day was fucking perfect. This is week four of Zach's ear infection. I persist in dragging my miserable three-year-old child back and forth to the doctor, who can't seem to figure out what in hell the problem is. If there is anything I dread more than waking up every morning, it is definitely a trip to the physician's office.

I sigh and roll my eyes while stirring the chili on the stove.

"Daddy's home!" Tiny feet clomp up the stairs, announcing the siege. Maya winds herself around one of Ethan's legs and Zach pulls at his waistband, demanding a hug.

"How are you feeling, little dude?" Ethan asks Zach as he swoops him up.

"Hurts." Zach points to his ear, then tucks it down against Ethan's shoulder.

"Stella, did Craig's office finally work you in?" Our regular family physician, Craig Washburn, who we love and know well, fled town to administer medicine in some remote third world country, so while they receive his outstanding service for free, we pay a premium for a woman who obviously didn't graduate first in her class. Figures. Until now, this kid has never had an ear infection. As soon as our doctor departs to spend a month half-way around the world, poof, Zach is sick.

"Yeah, finally. That idiot receptionist made the appointment for Thursday instead of today, even though our substitute doctor specifically told her she needed to see him today, so we ended up wasting over an hour. I'll be lucky if Zach didn't contract something worse in the waiting room."

So many people interview their physicians. Screw that. Interview their staff. Can the records chick spell your child's name? Can the appointment lady work the computer software? Will she occasionally call in prescriptions in a timely manner, and to the correct pharmacy?

Since Zach isn't recovering, in between appointments I deal with crappy receptionists. "Hmm, you haven't slept in how long? What if we give you an appointment in six weeks? Will you off yourself by then so we don't have to mess with you?" Or my personal favorite, "I thought I had a spot today, but the computer froze up. Now that I rebooted it, the first available appointment is next Thursday."

Those women are evil. They play favorites with the patients they like, but I generally don't fall into that category. Patients like me start calling three minutes before the office opens, and call every minute on the minute thereafter to ensure that we are the first phone call through. Yes, I have an opinion on whether or not he is seen today. Yes, when I call, I need a doctor now, not in two weeks, because we don't show up unless we're actually fucking sick.

Last Friday, during Zach's fourth appointment with the sub for this ongoing issue, she prescribed drops for the pain and promised, "If you make it through the weekend, I'll work you in on Monday to take a look at his ears again." I scheduled the appointment before I left the office. Obviously that was effective.

"So what did she say?" Ethan inquires. "Did she give him a different prescription to try?"

"What did she say?" I repeat, boiling inside at the memory. "She complained that his earwax blocks her view, as if I can dig down in his ear and pull it out. Isn't that her job?" I flop the wooden spoon onto the spoon rest by the pan, splattering my sweater with chili. Lovely. "Then she bitched about parents who overuse antibiotics, before finally writing him another prescription."

"Some patients do, though," Ethan sides with the sub, his words trailing off as I raise my eyebrows. Why can't he ever just agree with me?

"Seriously, Ethan? Why is it that more than three-quarters of the antibiotics manufactured go into our farm animals, encouraging resistant bacteria strains, and no one sees a problem with it, but physicians revolt when parents want to use them to help their children? Could it be that the parents aren't the ones causing the resistance problems but no one wants to tackle the real cause?"

"You're overreacting, Stella." He focuses his attention on the children, terminating our conversation. "Let's go build a fort before dinner, guys."

They tumble down the steps and I'm left in silence. Being in health care, he doesn't comprehend it. Ethan spends most of his working hours resenting patients. As manager for the endocrinology division, he blames the patients for their diabetes, judges them constantly for their lifestyles, and thinks most of them deserve their poor health because they don't live in the health-obsessed sphere where he resides. He is rarely sick and has never had a major illness. He truly believes that all illness can be prevented through diet and exercise. Endocrinology is the perfect throne from which to distribute his judgments.

At times I can see his point of view as our insurance expenses rise during benefit enrollment every year. I believe a healthy lifestyle is beneficial, but even people who eat clean and exercise faithfully still die at some point, which disproves his theory. I remind myself that he spends every day immersed in problem patients and many of those patients have no critical thinking or problem solving skills. He has to vent his frustrations somewhere.

Our house phone rings. I answer as I turn from the stove to retrieve crackers from the cupboard. The caller is a patient from Ethan's office, so I plod down the steps to find him. They never seem to distinguish that he is the manager, not a physician. Most nights and even some weekends, Ethan takes calls at home. Living in such a rural area, patients easily find our number.

I tap on the top of the fort to get Ethan's attention. He peers out and I mouth the word "patient". He nods his head in acceptance, extricates himself and retreats to the bedroom, phone in hand. As I return to the chili in the kitchen, his pacing footsteps creak above me.

Fifteen minutes pass before he returns the phone to the cradle. "What now?" I ask. "Another crisis?"

"Who knows. His wife has seen three different doctors in our office and doesn't even remember which medications she's supposed to take. I sent them to the ER and then paged the on-call and asked him to meet them there."

"That was nice of you," I compliment him, hoping he will provide more information that we can discuss. Even if I don't understand every nuance, I enjoy listening to Ethan's enthusiasm as he delves into the details of endocrinology. It reminds me how intelligent he actually is.

But Ethan is already halfway down the stairs. Over his shoulder, he explains, "It's my job. If the patients don't trust me, then we can't help them effectively." His statement is ironic since he flat out refuses to allow me to call our physician or to call him himself, even though we know Craig personally, I've been to his house to hang out with his wife, and we live next door to his in-laws. Maybe that shouldn't bother me, but it does.

Back in November, I took the kids to a paint-your-own-pottery shop to make Christmas gifts for my parents. They had a fantastic time, but at the end of the session, the leader asked the parents to set the pottery in a kiln that looked like a microwave oven covered in insulation.

Of course, as I was putting in Zach's painted dog statue, I smashed my finger against the side of the kiln. It hurt like hell. My finger started to swell and turn black and I could actually smell the burn. It was a miracle I didn't pass out. The woman running the shop scooted back to the kitchen for ice.

Maya and Zach both panicked, so I snuggled and comforted them with tears streaming down my face while frantically searching through my purse for my cell phone. While we iced my finger, I hit the speed dial for Ethan at work.

"Hello?" he answered.

"Ethan, it's me. I just burned my finger. Like, really burned it. I have both kids with me. Can you give Craig a call and ask what to do? You know if I call his office, I'll be stuck going round and round with the staff."

"You know I can't do that. I only call him directly to discuss patients that we share." Ethan sounded annoyed.

"Yes, and I am one of his patients. I'm sitting in a make-your-own-pottery studio with two crying children and a finger that smells like it might fall off. I'd tell you how much it hurts, but at this point I can't feel it at all. I can't imagine that's good. Please don't make me take the children to the emergency room to wait in line and sit for hours. If Craig thinks it needs attention, he can call down there and have someone waiting for me when I arrive." At this point, I was pleading. The thought of sitting in the emergency room with the kids overwhelmed me. We hadn't been home for hours and they were tired and hungry.

"No. I won't do it."

"Fine, I'll just call the office and see what they can do."

"No, Stella. Don't bother him. He'll be running between patients and trying to finish up his charting. Just go to the ER."

"Ethan, I don't want to go to the ER," I yelled, while yanking Zach away from a plate that stood perilously close to the edge of a low shelf. "Why are you more worried about Craig's schedule than you are about my finger?"

"I'm sorry, Stella. I have to go. My next meeting is starting in a few minutes and I need to grab Martin before it. I'll see you at home tonight." Ethan hung up.

I had no idea who Martin was. Ethan never offered to leave work or even walked down to the ER, though his office is in the same fucking building. I realized that whatever happened, no help would come from him. I loaded the kids into the van and cruised through McDonald's en route to the hospital so that I could at least purchase Happy Meals to provide both food and a toy for entertainment. I took the kids to the ER with me, and amazingly enough, they were well behaved—*and* we escaped in less than three hours.

Ethan was already home when we arrived, standing in the kitchen, covered in sweat, chugging a protein shake.

"You went to the gym?" I asked incredulously after sending the kids to their rooms in search of pajamas.

"Stella, I had an awful day. Martin, this consultant they brought in, demanded to see all of the office flowcharts and wanted me to present the work I've done on our accreditation to the board. He literally gave me fifteen minutes to prepare and that was when you called. By the time the performance was over, I had to decompress. You know I hate presenting material to the CEO." To him, the entire day is justified since everything worked out in the end.

"Yep, I had a pretty awful day too," I sniped, waving the giant wrap on my finger under his nose. "Too bad mine ended in the ER with two children and no support." I turned to gaze out the window, increasing the distance between us to examine the trees towering in our backyard. Ethan closed the gap and I almost relaxed into him, but as his hands grazed my hips and moved down my thighs, I flinched. "What are you doing?"

"I'm trying to be close to you," he sighed as he grabbed the sponge off the sink and wiped down our already clean kitchen counters to indicate his frustration.

He doesn't know how to process my emotions, so he physically grabs at me instead. When I rebuff him, he resorts to controlling his environment. He expects me to be so strong that I'm not allowed to be weak.

I needed encouragement. I needed to feel like he understood my pain and my isolation, for him to notice *my* universe, the one inside me. But instead, he groped me and cleaned the counters.

"I'm stuck," a muffled whine from upstairs interrupted our silence. With a deep breath, I fled from the room and helped the kids to bed, then went to bed myself without saying goodnight. Ethan never asked about my finger, despite the solution I had to soak it in twice a day.

That night we crossed a line we haven't come back from. We spend our evenings in a flurry of activity with Zach and Maya, but we don't ever really talk. I don't know what happens during the course of his day. He doesn't care what happens during mine.

I miss being intellectual. Nothing about being a stay at home mom is intellectual. I don't think I use even a half of one percent of my brain. Maybe that's why I prepare my own taxes and argue over contracts; they give me something to think about other than preschool song lyrics. Sometimes I wish Ethan would just talk to me, tell me about his day, relate funny stories from work, or at least listen to my crazy mundane ones. But he doesn't want to hear my stories. Hell, I guess I wouldn't, either. Most days are one small variation of another.

Inside, I'm slowly dying. It isn't that I miss my career so much; I just miss other people recognizing me as a person who is worth something. I worked for the first two years of Maya's life. Ethan and I rotated schedules, sharing the work and the childcare. The schedule was hard, but we managed. I loved my job and I was good at it. Then came Zach. He came into the world with a spreadsheet of medical issues. My attempt to manage his health and work full-time overwhelmed me. Customers called me with immediate concerns during medical appointments that I couldn't escape. Ethan expected me to modify my schedule to accommodate all of the children's needs while he never deviated from his path. I felt guilty constantly about scheduling conflicts. I couldn't give one hundred percent while taking business calls at home because the children distracted me. When I was busy at work, I stressed over trying to squeeze in the physician visits that Zach desperately needed. Ethan and I argued constantly and eventually decided to move so that I could stay home.

No one warns you of the flip side when you bravely pursue your dreams and achieve them. I earned my engineering degree. I was the first woman engineer in my company and the youngest, and only female, manager. I achieved more before thirty than some people do in a lifetime. Then I chose to switch it, stay home, raise kids, and spend my time supervising preschool outings and preparing Valentine's Day crafts. Being home with the children eased my guilt, but it doesn't fulfill me. No matter how much I try, I can't become one of those women who is fulfilled and happy to live through her husband and children. Somehow, it still is not enough.

"Dinner," I call, ladling the chili into bowls, placing them around the table, and covering the kids' chairs with towels. Let the mess-making begin.

Ethan arrives first, creeping through the kitchen. "We're playing a game. They have to find me. You, I'll play with later," he whispers as he pinches my ass, winks, and ducks down behind the table, camouflaged by the towels on the chairs. That's my husband, shooting down meaningful conversation at every turn but more than happy to play a game and grab my ass.

After dinner, I bathe Maya and snuggle Zach to distract him from the pain in his ear. Ethan wanders to the den instead of offering assistance since playtime is over. He cleans up the fort and checks the score of a game to tune us out. By the time I return, he is asleep on the sofa. Maybe if I'm lucky, he'll stay that way and give me a break tonight from his relentless physical expectations. I'm not in the mood to be played with. So I shuffle to the computer, alone again, wondering if I'm going to be stuck in this purgatory forever.

Chapter 4 ~ July

Since Ethan took his job two years ago, his boss has been pressing him to go back to school to work toward his MBA. I was glad he accepted when they offered again this spring. It means a lot more work for him and even less help around the house for me, but hopefully it will secure his place in the hospital administration.

This weekend, MBA homework flew out the window. Theo, one of the twins next door, and Ethan devised a project to build a giant retaining wall in the middle of the yard. Since our front yard is sliding perilously close to our garage, we do require a retaining wall, but I don't approve of the execution. They asked me to review the plans and I downright refused. I'm trying to register Zach for preschool and finish all the paperwork for Kindergarten registration for Maya. I can guarantee he doesn't know the name of either of their schools. To help him, I'd need time to design the wall in detail and calculate the stresses and drainage. I'm a bit of a perfectionist. And my degree is biomedical, so I'd need to do a little research because, contrary to popular belief, possessing an engineering degree does not indicate the ability to design any random thing instantaneously.

Ethan, however, has no interest in waiting. "Theo says we can build it this weekend."

"This weekend? Doesn't that seem a bit rushed? Does Theo have any idea what he's doing?"

Ethan pulls out a hand-drawn pseudo-schematic and explains everything they plan to do. They'll dig the trench by hand. Theo has some distant family member that can pour the concrete for the footer and another one to bring gravel to fill around the drain. That Newlan family is like the mafia. They always have an uncle who will show up and work on just about anything under the table for cash.

"So what's the catch?" Ethan has the gleam in his eye that means some expectation of me hasn't surfaced yet.

"Well, I have a marketing paper to write. I was hoping you might be willing to outline it for me while I start digging the trench with Theo."

Instead of upsetting me, his request flatters me. He knows I can write a marketing paper and it will probably be better than the one he'd produce. Lord knows I miss using my brain. So I strut down to the computer, ready to tackle online versus print marketing strategies and write a comparison. I sit down to begin mapping my ideas and hear the door slam as Ethan scurries out to start digging.

"He hit me!" A scream echoes from the basement. Crap. Zach and Maya have been playing so nicely that I actually forgot they were still inside. How in the world am I supposed to write with all that noise?

"In three minutes Scooby Doo will come on," I announce and they file into the den.

Maya sprints to the TV as fast as her stubby legs can move her. She grabs the blue fold-out chair with a fervor usually reserved for birthday cake and catapulting off the sofa, and pulls it over until it is point three millimeters from the TV screen.

Zach's close behind her. He watches her set up the chair and then pushes her off it. She waits a second to make sure I'm looking, puckers up, and then starts to fake cry. "Mommy, he took my chair."

"Push him off," I reply. Wait a minute, did I just say that? Yep, I sure did. Shit. I can guarantee she'll tell Ethan when he comes back inside. Do I really have to chase this four-year-old terror around and tell him no every three minutes? Is it wrong to teach her to stick up for herself?

"What?" She gapes at me like I just told her she could jump out of a moving car. "But, Mommy, I'm not supposed to push people."

Damn it. I hop up off the sofa, pick Zach up, who immediately starts sniveling, and allow her to sit back in the chair. The Scooby Doo song starts to play.

I put Zach in time out. He fiddles quietly with his fingers and behaves. When I dismiss him, he shuffles over to the toy table and quietly rummages through the toys.

Thank God. I race to the kitchen and just pop the top off my root beer when I hear Robby, the incredibly loud and annoying dancing robot that we received from my in-laws, fire up at full volume.

"Mommy, I can't hear," Maya yells.

I tromp back down the steps to remove the offending toy. "You can play with him upstairs or come to the kitchen with me, okay, Zach? Your sister can't hear Scooby Doo."

"No." Zach glares at me and tears up.

"Mommy, I can't hear," Maya whines again, this time jacking up the TV volume.

"Zach, please stop." I pick up a puzzle, hoping it will encourage him to look through his toys again.

"No." Smack. Freaking Fergus the train, a Christmas present from this past year, just hit me in the face.

"Zach, no throwing," I say as I pick up Fergus and put it on top of the mantle. Whack. Salty whooshes by my head and hits a lamp before joining Fergus on the mantle. Harold flies across the room and bounces off the coffee table.

Damn it. "Do not throw!" I pick up all the trains and dump them on top of the mantle. Zach marches over, picks up a small toy radio, and throws it as hard as he can on the floor.

"No," he screams again.

"Mommy, I can't hear." Maya cranks the TV louder still.

I think I'm going to lose my mind. Do people really have more than two children? Is it intentional? Do they like them?

I flip off the TV and growl, "Upstairs," with clenched teeth. I pick up Zach, holding him like a football so that he can't kick or hit me while I move him, and wrangle his flailing body up the steps. On the way into his room, he whacks his head on the doorframe. I swear he does it on purpose.

Maya whines and cries, "But I didn't do anything wrong," in her most pitiful, woe-is-me voice.

I stomp out the front door. Ethan and Theo are knee deep in their trench. Tad watches from the sidelines, looking amused.

"How is the paper going?" asks Ethan.

"Paper, really?" I say with as much sarcasm as I can muster. "Could you not hear the screaming through the walls?"

The boys chuckle. Obviously, they heard most of it.

"We're the poster children for birth control," I snap. "You guys should pay attention because, believe me, you don't actually want one of those." That stops them. Theo looks a little sick. I always pegged him as the wild one.

"What are you writing about?" Tad tries to defuse my anger.

"Some marketing crap comparing print versus online concepts."

"Did you pick a company?"

"Did it sound like I had time to pick a company?"

"I'll help you out if you want," he offers. "I'm not in the mood to dig."

"There you go," Ethan interjects. "Now you even have help. It'll be done in no time." He turns back and resumes his digging. I halt and watch him. The ropy muscles in his forearms flex as he heaves the shovel deeper into the trench and sweat glistens down his bare back, leaving dirt trails. His body tenses as he pulls the handle back, his concentration intently focused on one square foot of metal. His physical exertion draws me in; I remember how I felt watching him run up and down the basketball court in college. I want to grab Ethan's hand and lead him into the house, up the steps to our room—

"You ready?" Tad follows me into the house, where it is strangely silent.

"Give me a minute," I whisper over my shoulder and creep up the steps. Zach has fallen asleep. Thank God. Maya lies on her floor with a pile of books and looks like she isn't far from joining him. I tiptoe back down the steps.

"At least they're quiet," he says. "But you're right, there's no way I want kids."

"Uh, duh," I retort. "You're what, eighteen? How many kids your age actually want kids?"

He grins.

"So what are your plans anyway?" I haven't really talked to him since before his graduation.

"Army," he responds without hesitation.

Why am I not surprised? This kid is so regimented it's the only logical choice. His daily uniform consists of black pants and a button-down shirt; I've never seen him leave the house in a pair of jeans. His mannerisms are precise and focused. His hair is already shorn, prepared for his career well in advance.

"So what are you going to do?"

"Computers, I hope. I'm going to school in St. Louis to be a computer engineer, but I'll go ROTC and straight into the Army afterwards. I can't wait to get out of here. I hate this town."

"So that's your thing? Computers?"

"Yep. If you need any help with yours, feel free to ask."

"Excellent, because the blue screen of death constantly pops up on my laptop. Now, let's pick a company."

"Select something you know well," he suggests as I shuffle through our magazine basket, evaluating candidates. "It will make the entire project go faster."

"Obviously." Why am I collaborating on a marketing paper with a kid who just graduated from high school? "Ding ding. I found a winner," I announce, turning from the basket and waving the catalog in his general direction.

"I've never even heard of that company before," Tad attempts to dismiss my choice as he plucks a Global Computer Supply catalog from the mix.

"I am not comparing computers," I grumble, snatching the catalog from his hand and tossing it back on the top of the pile. "You said to pick something I know well, so you just eliminated *your* top choice." I wiggle my Hannah Andersson catalog again. "I am intimately familiar with this one due to my children's obsessive fixation with avoiding contact with elastic."

"You're the boss," he says as he shrugs. Our chairs almost touch as we pull them up alongside the computer so we can both see the monitor. I open the website while he flips through the catalog. Then we trade without speaking, coordinating our effort easily without discussion. It is almost as if he already knows that I have to work in silence, gathering my thoughts before I can release them. He appears to be doing the same. The keyboard clacks quietly as I list my observations; his pencil scratches a notepad almost continuously. The lull in the conversation is easy and relaxed, with no pressure to fill in the blanks.

After a while, Tad closes the magazine and glances at me, indicating he is ready to proceed.

"Yes?"

"Can I read your thoughts now?"

"Yours first," I reply. "No plagiarizing off my list."

He swivels in his seat, shifting his weight closer to me while angling the notepad so that I can't see what he's written and reads his list out loud.

"Not bad." Tad's insight takes me aback. His collaboration is that of an equal, not someone inserting an uninformed opinion, and definitely not that of a high school kid. "The only thing you missed is that the catalog pictures are designed to sell happy children. The website pictures aren't. Maybe on the web, they don't want to be mistaken for a child traffickers."

"How can you even joke about that?"

Tad snaps his fingers to command my attention. I should probably be offended, but he challenges me. He doesn't even faintly resemble any guy I knew in high school. The boys I knew copied my homework and stole Wild Turkey from their parents.

"Sorry I offended you, but is there a reason you're so upset by a sarcastic comment?" Tad delves into detail, reciting statistics and atrocities. I interrupt occasionally, but mostly I listen, mesmerized. I can't remember the last time I spoke with anyone about a truly important topic.

He finally answers my question. "So, no, there is no reason and I'm not upset. I just say what I think. The abuse of children isn't anything to joke about, even if you do occasionally want to bury your own brats in the backyard." He wags his finger as if he's scolding me, indicating the serious part of the conversation is over.

"Better watch where you put that finger." I laugh as Tad shoots me a look of feigned annoyance, then pretends he didn't hear me.

He leans over my shoulder to review my list, and we return to dissecting the strategy as we record our similarities and differences. As we near the end of our comparison, I begin to fidget. "Do you want a Coke or something?" I ask.

"Nah," he responds.

"So why are you still here helping me? Don't you have something more exciting to do? I can't imagine that writing a paper with a tired mom is an exciting way for you to spend Saturday afternoon."

"We help people," he says, his face serious. "My parents expect us to."

27

Greeneville is definitely different from Nashville, where we used to live. I loved the city. I loved the anonymity. I loved the fact that no one was in my business or really cared what I was doing. I loved the energy from the traffic and the people and the life. In the city my friends were diverse, but they were all educated, open-minded people. I received an infusion of life just from being around people who loved and accepted me for who and what I am. But no one ever offered to help us with anything there without being well compensated.

In Greeneville, we are members of the Country Club and have all the right superficial friends. I'm in Junior League. Ethan attends Rotary meetings and leads the board at the YMCA. But we haven't broken the surface with anyone, although there are ten people I could call to watch the kids if I needed it. No real problems exist here, just a tide, an undercurrent that sucked me away from myself.

"So I guess that's part of living in a small town, huh?" When we moved here, I never anticipated the culture would be so different.

"Not really. Generally it's just a bunch of people who talk about you behind your back and spread rumors," he tells me. "But my dad makes us help everyone. And if we're over here, at least we don't have to do chores for him."

"Good enough for me," I answer. Tad's father, Terry, is a prison guard. We say hi across the driveway occasionally, but our conversations are limited. Terry and Tracey are closer to our age and are raising children just as we are; theoretically, they should be our friends. We don't dislike them, but no commonalities jump through to span the gap to friendship. Oddly, Ethan and I relate more easily to Tad and Theo.

"So you can let me know if you need anything done," he adds. "I can stop by during the days to help with whatever."

The front door opens and Ethan yells, "Can you bring us some waters?" Thanks, honey. Why don't you just use a bullhorn? The kids would be more likely to sleep through that.

"Can we come down?" Maya's up.

"Bweak time over?" Zach calls.

"The monsters are restless." I peer over the keyboard. "Time to call it a day. Thanks again, Tad, for all your help."

"Anytime," he says, looking me in the eye. "I mean it."

PART III

2008

Chapter 5 ~ January

It's three forty-three a.m. Zach woke me up again. I don't know what I'm doing. This is the third time tonight. Maya's a sleeper. Zach isn't. Is there nothing on this earth I can do that will make that child sleep through the night? I haven't had a decent night's sleep in three years.

So here I sit. God, I hate him. I glare into his little screaming face and wonder over and over what I did to deserve this misery. I remember when I had the kids everyone told me how lucky I was. And what a blessing they are. There must be something wrong with me, because I don't see it. My brain must not be wired right.

People rocking their babies in the middle of the night in the movies are happy. The baby snuggles up and coos softly. The mother bows her head like she appreciates every second. What the fuck is that? And why don't I have it? My kid screams and I want to throw him out the damn window. I'm tired. I'm so fucking tired I don't know my name or what day of the week it is. The inane conversation and arguments with a six year old over whether Cinderella rode a damn horse or a pony exasperate me.

Does everyone feel this way? Do they count the minutes until their kids go to bed? Do they dread waking up in the morning, required to waste another day singing itsy bitsy spider? How do they keep from just driving off a cliff? I imagine it countless times per month. The feeling of flying and then nothing. I would do anything to feel nothing. Right now, all I feel is pain and overwhelming exhaustion. Now I know what prisoners of war feel like. Constant sleep deprivation. Constant stupid questioning over and over. It is just like being a parent with children who talk incessantly and don't sleep.

Zach's breathing evens out but I'm scared to move. He traps me in his little twin bed, precariously balanced on the edge. I inch away from him, slowly pulling back the covers, ready to make my escape. Smack. That freaking kid just rolled over and hit me in the nose. "Waa." Shit. That is what I get for moving. "Waa," he screams. Damn it, where did his favorite stuffed cow go?

A light pops on. "Mommy, I can't sleep. Zach woke me up." Maya peers around the corner into Zach's room.

I wonder what incident set off the lady who drowned all her kids in the bathtub. Was this it? The breaking point where she said, "Line up. Mommy is giving you a bath"? Am I going to turn into her? Is that where this is going?

I calm myself, snuggle both kids into Maya's larger queen-sized bed, and tell their favorite story, the one that uses their names as the characters. They fall asleep together almost immediately and, finally, I can go back to bed.

So I return to my now cold spot in the middle of the bed, thinking, "Now I can sleep." But, nope, not happening. I wind my arms around Ethan's warm furry chest, trying to match my breathing to his. Pressed against him, a distance gapes between us. Even right next to me, he isn't here for me when I need him.

Last night, when the kids were finally in bed, I returned a call to my best friend from high school who was just diagnosed with leukemia. After we disconnected, Ethan swept into the den and wanted me to play Scrabble with him. I was depressed, upset, and needed a friend to talk to, but he wanted to play Scrabble. And he was serious. In nine years of marriage, I've won precisely one game of Scrabble and that was after a dental surgery while he was still partially under anesthesia. He is so detached from my reality that he thinks a fucking game of Scrabble is going to make it all better. I guess I should appreciate him taking time out of his busy schedule to acknowledge that I do exist, but somehow I'm not grateful. I need someone to listen, to connect with, and to tell me it will be okay. He expects me to be as independent and self-assured as he is. I'm not. Somehow, this relationship became a competition to see who needs who the least. He always wins. And I always lose.

I want him to *care*. Being left alone with Zach in the middle of the night is nothing new. Hell, Ethan left me alone when I was in labor with him. I delivered in the same hospital where Ethan was working. My water broke three weeks early, on the day Ethan was scheduled to present his office expansion proposal to the board. In the beginning, I didn't mind being alone because I figured the whole thing would take a while. His sister Lisa called off work to supervise Maya. He worked all day. I was alone when my doctor inserted my IV. I was alone for the epidural. When my doctor panicked over a test and called in colleagues to consult, I was alone. Ethan popped in around dinner time, stayed two hours, and then became angry when I asked him to stay instead of going home to sleep. He still left to shower and change clothes. Upon his return, he completed his paperwork for the week of leave he'd scheduled for after the birth and then rearranged meetings on his laptop instead of holding my hand.

The next morning, since my slow progression wasn't holding his attention, he went out to brunch with his co-workers, twenty-eight hours into my labor, when I was eight centimeters dilated. I paged him when the time came to push. Literally. Most husbands run red lights and fall over themselves for the birth of their child. My husband eats brunch with other women.

"Waa."

Shit. I elbow Ethan. "Can you grab him? He's in Maya's room, which means they'll both be awake. I'm exhausted. I've already been up three times with him."

"In a minute," Ethan responds, drawing a deep breath and tightening the covers around him as he rolls over.

My eyes close while my mind ticks off the seconds and Zach's wailing amplifies. "Ethan." My fists clinch and the pressure in my jaw increases, slicing the frustration that claws up my throat into silence.

Ethan's body jumps and his breathing evens into a light snore. He fell asleep. That jackass just fell asleep while Zach is fucking screaming. I want to kick him, yell at him, and force him to bare the brunt of this overwhelming mess that he helped me create. I'm so angry I want to punch a wall and scream. Instead, I rise and trudge back down the hall.

I doze off lightly while resettling Zach in his own room. When I finally return to our bed and collapse, the clock approaches time for Ethan's early-morning run. "Morning," he murmurs, as he rolls to his side and pulls me against him, grinding himself into my back. "Rough night?"

I am so furious that I can't breathe. He wants me to be simple. He wants me not to think too much, not to expect too much, and to take whatever he offers as enough. I'm supposed to be his best friend, laugh at his jokes, and comfort him when he is upset. I'm supposed to placate his friends, provide sex on demand, and maintain an affectionate, happy mask while I juggle the kids. He likes the idea of our children, but refuses to take the responsibility for the decisions that are required to raise them. Instead of helping with them, he acts like one.

His fingers travel the peaks of my breasts as he nuzzles into my shoulder. How does he not see me? He wants all the good parts of a relationship without taking the responsibility that comes along with it. Does he really not know that I resent him, or does he just pretend that he doesn't see it so that I am the crazy one? No matter what I need, he seems to go out of his way to make sure he doesn't give it to me, even if I specifically ask for it. Why is it now my responsibility to meet his need? I'm not his fucking parent. I have enough kids as it is to take care of; I don't need another one.

"Ethan, I've been up all night. Not now. I'm exhausted."

"But I miss you." His words grate against me like the whine of an annoying child. He misses me because of his own fucking schedule. He comes home late with no concern for the inconvenience it causes me. He might tell me he'll be home at five thirty and then walk through the door at quarter to seven because he stopped off at the gym. He plays poker one night of almost every weekend, but I schedule my nights out weeks in advance because he expects me to avoid conflicts with his activities. He might not miss me if he occasionally came home. But he owes nothing, does nothing, and supports nothing. In his mind, his financial contribution is enough. The problem is that he completely neglects our relationship to keep himself happy. And I detach from him more and more with each disappointment. Soon there may be nothing at all to hold us together.

One hand travels down and begins to gently massage my thigh, working its way inward. "You used to love sex in the morning," he says. "The kids will sleep for a while now. It's our turn."

I know this is his way of trying to connect with me. I know that, to him, sex is the one remaining tie that binds us together as we grope through the dark, trying to keep our hold on each other. My white flag flies as I accept the inevitable. "I guess." I roll to him and allow his hands to wander as I set my mind adrift.

Chapter 6 ~ July

During the summers, my sister-in-law Lisa watches the kids one morning a week for me so that I can take a break. I generally spend this time running, swimming laps in our pool, or grocery shopping, since those three things are almost impossible to do with two children in tow. I'm ready to run when she shows up. We walk into the den and chat for a few minutes because the kids are still sleeping. When I walk back to grab my iPod and leave, I see a strange looking car idling in my driveway.

Most people won't come down it due to its steep slope. No delivery van or truck ever attempts it, and even most of our good friends park at a spot we've paved up near the road and walk down. I don't recognize the person in this car. It is an older, beat up, two-door red Chevy Cavalier. I'm no car expert, but I happen to know this particular model.

The engine revs, and the car shoots about half way up the drive before it stops and rolls back down again. I'm terrified that this guy is going to crash into my living room. I open the front door and fly out.

"Excuse me," I yell as I approach the car.

An extremely overweight man drives the car; his stomach protrudes below the hem of his too-short T-shirt. On his head, he wears a floppy straw hat and sunglasses. A dark mustache and beard cover his face. He bends over and hand-cranks down the passenger side window. He doesn't say a word, just looks at me. The car looks like he lives in it. The ceiling upholstery bubbles and falls in areas; trash and debris surround him. Wires hang out of the dash where the stereo obviously used to be. A terrifying feeling of déjà vu sweeps over me, bringing memories of another red Cavalier, one from long ago. I am in the front passenger seat, and there's a body pressing down on me, large hands inching up my thigh—I slam the door on them. The hairs on the back of my neck stand up. This doesn't feel right.

"Is there something I can help you with, sir?" I ask. "If you're having car trouble, I'll be happy to call a tow truck for you."

"Nope. Be out of here in a minute," he replies.

I watch as he starts up and then rolls back down my driveway another three times.

"I'm sorry," I interrupt again since the window is still down, "but can I ask how you ended up at the bottom of my driveway?" Our street is a quiet one. Since it is only about one and a half lanes wide, vehicles that meet going opposite directions tend to move slowly and very few people use it as a cut-through. There is no logical way to end up at the bottom of my driveway.

"I came down from over there," he motions to my neighbor's yard.

Not the Newlans', but the neighbor on the other side, our doctor's in-laws. Now that he points that direction, I see the tire tracks. He drove across the Johnsons' driveway, down at an angle through my front yard, and somehow managed to avoid my garage, two flower beds, and my sister-in-law's vehicle. Thank God the kids were inside.

As he proceeds to ramp up and roll down my driveway again and again, I withdraw into the house. The kids are awake now and watch with interest through the window.

"Lisa," I say, "please take them downstairs and keep them there. Something weird is going on here. If he hits the house, I don't want the kids in the living room." I run up the steps, grab the wooden bat out from under our bed, and place it by the front door. At the same time, I dial the police and explain the situation. They claim they're on their way.

I walk back outside and, right in front of this guy, record his license plate number in a notebook. "The police are on their way to help you," I inform him before bolting back into the house. I sit on the sofa to nervously watch and wait. Half an hour passes. Finally, the red Cavalier disappears out of our driveway. I remember that my sister-in-law is on the clock, and I need to pay her for this entire time, although I'm stuck sitting here waiting for the police to show up. After waiting an hour, I call back. The officer who answers informs me that they drove by, didn't see anyone in the drive, and didn't bother to stop. Lovely. Thanks for serving and protecting. I ask if they would like the license plate number of the car to record the incident and she supposedly takes it down, but my guess is she humors me so she can hang up the phone.

When Ethan comes home, I describe the story in detail. This is the second time I've been home and experienced a situation where I wished I had more protection. The first time, two men drove into our back yard and dumped trash. Being me, I stomped down the hill with baby Zach on my hip and ordered them to leave, but when I think back, they could have easily raped or murdered me.

Ethan has resisted owning firearms for our entire marriage. I think he's scared of them. Or maybe he's just scared that I'll shoot him. My dad never hunted, but we still owned a rifle and a few handguns. He is an accountant and travels during tax season, and my mom always said she felt more comfortable knowing that she had some way to protect us. I never perceived the guns as a threat. They were kept locked up and separate from us, but never hidden. I knew where they were. Ethan never had that. His family never owned a gun when he was growing up.

After I finish my story, Ethan looks tense.

"So are you going to finally let me have one?" I ask. "I'd feel a lot more comfortable being here alone with the kids if I did. And although you don't travel a ton for work, you do attend a couple conferences a year, not to mention all of the weekends you disappear to athletic events."

"What are you going to get? I mean, are you just going to go buy one? Do you even know what to do with it?"

"No, but I know that there are classes. With those new concealed carry laws, I think there are classes all over the place. I bet the Newlans would know. Would you care if I ask them to recommend a class? Then you can decide."

"Okay," Ethan finally acquiesces. "I'm not comfortable with this, but go ahead and try it out. See if you can find a class so that we don't have to buy anything immediately."

A huge wave of relief pours through me. I don't feel threatened often, but when I do, I want the power to control the situation.

Monday morning after the kids' swimming lessons, I pull into our driveway still thinking about it. I didn't bump into any of the Newlans over the weekend and I'm not brave enough to walk up to their house. They own a couple of huge Dobermans that I'm more comfortable with from a distance. This morning, however, Tad's legs protrude from beneath his hand-me-down Corolla, surrounded by tools.

"Hey," I walk his direction after releasing the kids to run through the backyard with strict orders to stay away from the pool. "Did the wicked witch drop a car on you?"

"What?" he asks as he rolls out from under the car and turns down the music that pumps out of the speakers.

"I asked if the wicked witch dropped a car on you."

"No, just replacing my brakes and rotors."

"You do that yourself? Hell, I don't even change my own oil."

"Yep. Change the oil myself too. Working on the car gives me something to think about for a while. Theo sits inside playing video games and it drives me insane. Out here, he leaves me alone. So, do you need something?"

"I want to learn to shoot. I know you guys do all that stuff. Can you recommend someone who offers classes or something?"

"I can," he says. "I'll give you a card for the guy I took the concealed carry class from. But you don't have a gun, do you?"

"No. Actually, I've never even held one. But I want to learn so maybe one of these days I can own one. I finally talked Ethan into it, so I have to find something quick before he changes his mind."

"You've never held one?" He looks at me like I'm a circus oddity. I guess here in Appalachia, I probably am. "Really?"

"Nope. Ethan isn't comfortable with them."

"Well, I can give you his card, but he only runs the classes a few times a year," he says. I must look disappointed, because he adds, "But I'll be happy to teach you. We shoot almost every weekend. You could come along. I'll bring a bunch of different guns and you can try them all and see what you like."

"Really? You'd do that?"

"Sure. You available this Saturday?"

"I think so. Let me run it by Ethan and I'll let you know." A scream from the bottom of the hill cuts our conversation short. Zach lies on his back underneath a tree, screaming. "Gotta go," I say and sprint toward the bottom of the hill. I hear the music crank back up by the time I get to my son.

Nothing is actually wrong with the drama king, of course. "Maya pinched me." He gives me a smug smile when I stand above him.

"Let's go," I roll my eyes. Dirt covers their swimsuits. "I'll hose you guys off in front of the house." They holler with glee and dance up the hill.

***

Ethan is brushing his teeth before bed when I decide to broach the issue. "Tad offered to teach me to shoot. He mentioned something about Saturday. What's on your schedule for the weekend?"

"I'm playing cards with Mark on Friday night," Ethan's response is garbled through the toothpaste. He spits, then continues, "No plans for Saturday. I was hoping to spend some time in the pool since I never get to swim during the week. Oh, but I did register for a 10K on Sunday morning."

"So that means Saturday is free? I can go?"

"Sure, that works." He is pleased because he thinks it will assuage me and allow him to avoid spending any money or putting any effort into fixing my problem.

"Great. I'll let Tad know tomorrow. Oh, and don't forget Zach is allergic to all the sunscreens in the bag now. You have to use the special one with his name on it that makes him look like a ghost. And don't let Maya take the reflective goggles. He has to use them or he gets a headache."

"He'll remind me, Stella."

"I know he will. He'll scream when his skin burns from the chemical spray or cry under the umbrella when his head hurts. I'd prefer to prevent that if possible."

"Maybe you should just stay home." The shift happens immediately. Ethan realizes that I'll be gone all day, which traps him at home with the kids and forces him to be the responsible one.

"I can leave you a list. It isn't that hard, Ethan. Sunscreen. Goggles.

I'll write it down and put it on the counter so you can't miss it." Concern radiates from Ethan's face and his arms cross in front of him.

Time to tap into my powers of persuasion. I step back for a moment, hold his gaze, and pull my tank off over my head. I cock my eyebrow in challenge, then push his old boxers I was planning to sleep in over my hipbones and let them fall.

Ethan's eyes widen. I approach him directly, nip only once at his collar bone, and drop to my knees. I flick my tongue through his trail of hair as I unbutton his shorts and dive in as his eyes close and his frame drapes against the sink.

I tease and manipulate him. But after a while, my jaw aches. Hairs entwine my tongue and I stifle the urge to gag. He builds toward crescendo, larger, deeper, as my revulsion increases and I count off the strokes until this ends. In one motion, I rotate away from him and bend over the sink. He frantically swallows the bait, the mirror pushing him over the edge as he watches himself cross the finish line.

I opted for the shortcut, but my mission is complete.

"Better?" I ask while grabbing my toothbrush.

"Have fun Saturday," he says.

I can talk that man into almost anything if I ask naked.

Chapter 7 ~ July

Saturday morning arrives and I wake up early. I'm supposed to be over at the Newlans' house at nine. Tad told me to wear long pants, which makes sense, but means I'll sweat like crazy since the July days grow progressively hotter and longer. I select a pair of jeans and then rummage through my T-shirts. Every single one of them either billows on me like a tent or boasts some stain or smudge reminiscent of a preschool art project or afternoon in the park. What can I wear? A couple of my old tees from before I had kids might be appropriate, but most of them are so tight that I'll look like I'm interviewing for a job at Hooters. Finally, I find a fitted tee from a U2 concert that Ethan and I saw on our second anniversary. It fits and the dark pattern will camouflage any stains when I sweat. Perfect.

When I finally escape after throwing breakfast in the kids' general direction, Tad is already loading the car. "Do you have eye and ear protection?" he asks.

"Nope," I respond. I used to, back when I worked. Now the only ear protection I require is a giant pillow over my head to allow me to sleep through his brother's crazy music in the middle of the night.

"You can grab some in the garage," he motions at a group of toolboxes.

"Specifically where?"

"I'll show you." I follow him. Their garage is crammed with so many tools and random half-finished projects that it could never house an automobile. I'm so busy looking around that when Tad stops to open a drawer in one of the storage units, I walk straight into him.

"Sorry," I mumble as he turns around. He isn't three inches from me and I can feel his breath.

"You guys ready?" Tad's dad calls.

"Yep." Tad grabs some earplugs and safety glasses, tosses them to me, and we walk back out to his Corolla. His dad sits shotgun, looking around impatiently. I guess that means he's going with us. As I climb in the backseat, I can't decide if I'm glad or disappointed.

On the way to the range, we swing by and pick up Terry's friend Kevin, who wants to try out his new gun. It's like a shooting party.

When we arrive at the range, we're the only people there. It's private and Terry has connections with the owner. We stand in a clearing in the middle of nowhere. I am the only woman, surrounded by three men and a lot of firearms. Although I'm intimidated and nervous, the attention excites me.

Terry pops the trunk and for the first time I see the array of firepower they chose to bring along. There are probably twelve guns, ranging from a small .22 to a rifle. Innumerable boxes contain all sizes and calibers of ammunition. The information overloads me. How in the world do you ever figure out what goes with what?

Kevin and Terry set up pizza boxes as targets in random spots, load up, and shoot. I have no idea what I'm supposed to do.

"Why don't you start with this one?" Tad hands me a Walther P-22. "It's small and light. Then we can work up to larger ones to see what you feel the most comfortable with."

"Sounds perfect," I say.

"Do you know how to switch the safety off?"

The blank look on my face must say it all, because he ejects the magazine out of the bottom of the gun, hands it to me, and picks up a revolver. "This is the frame," he begins, gesturing toward the gun like a game show host presenting a prize package. "Can you show me the barrel?"

My index finger taps the front of the gun. "I'm not a complete moron." I sigh.

"Okay, Miss Know-It-All. Where is the ejector rod on the gun I'm holding?"

Silence. No idea. And he isn't giving me any help. His eyes are completely serious and locked onto mine, challenging me to question his superiority.

"What is the difference between a single-action and double-action revolver? Actually, do you even know the difference between a revolver and a semi-automatic? Can you tell me the components of a cartridge? Are rimfire and center-fire cartridges interchangeable?"

"I surrender. You win. I know nothing and you are the supreme gun master. So just impart your knowledge and stop the harassment," I huff.

Tad proceeds to give me a fifteen minute overview of the different gun parts and how they work. His intricacy in the explanation conveys a passion for details. He then moves on to safety procedures. By the time he's done, I'm confident. I think I can do this. Tad places me in position in front of the first target.

"Whenever you're ready," he says. Now the others stop and watch me. Wonderful. I'll probably hit a tree.

I take aim, point, and shoot. The gun jumps as the sound of the shot, muffled by my hearing protection, reverberates through the air. I didn't hit a tree, but I didn't really hit the target, either. I did manage to clip the pizza box. After a few more practice rounds, I start to improve. The bullet still doesn't connect anywhere near the center, but I'm a little more consistent and at least closer to the bulls-eye.

I move from target to target, refining my aim. When I feel comfortable

A Thousand Tiny Cracks

with the .22, Tad takes it and hands me a .357 to try. We continue this way; he selects and loads the weapons while I take them all for test runs. I work through five different guns, but I really love that first Walther the best. I like how it feels in my hands.

Terry and Kevin do the same thing, trading off guns and rotating targets. As I finish up with a .45, Tad approaches me from behind and pauses.

"You want to try mine?" he asks.

His looks huge. The recoil from the .45 I currently struggle with hurts my shoulder. "What is it?"

"It's a nine millimeter," he tells me. "It probably has close to the same kick as the .45. Come try it. I'll help you."

Terry and Kevin have moved back across the field to the car. They lean on the bumper with the trunk open, talking.

"Okay, sure, I guess," I stutter.

Tad escorts me to the first target. He hands me his gun and steps back behind me. The gun is really heavy. When I pull the trigger, the barrel jumps and I miss the pizza box entirely.

"This one is way too big and heavy for me," I complain.

"Give it a chance," he says, moving closer to me. "You might like it." He's right behind me now. I can feel his chest press into my back as his arms circle me to help me stabilize the weapon. We're both sweaty, but I'm so aware of him touching me that it doesn't cross my mind.

"My shirt is a bit wet," he says. "Sorry about that."

"Yeah, I'm a little wet too." Then I'm silent. I might pass out. I think that statement might not have come out exactly as I intended.

He chuckles in my ear. "Now pull the trigger," he says. I do. The recoil presses me tightly back against him. The bullet flies straight through the middle of the bulls-eye. "See," he says, "you can do it. You just need the right teacher."

Tad steps back and I hear Terry and Kevin approach. They're ready to head for home, which is exactly where I need to go. We pick up bullet casings and pack everything into the car. On the drive back, my stomach growls. It's almost three in the afternoon, and none of us have eaten.

"Want to order pizza?" asks Terry.

We all three chorus "Yes" in agreement and Terry calls in the order so we can pick it up on the way back into town.

They clean their guns in the Newlans' garage. Tad tutors me on the Walther, showing me how to break it down. It is still my favorite. Terry and Kevin disappear into the house to examine some specialty gun cabinet that Terry just built. Tad and I are left in the garage alone and both of us are done cleaning and reassembling the guns, so we pile plates with pizza and flop in the corner.

I'm out of superficial conversation, so I steer him toward a hopefully benign topic. "Since you shoot all the time, and have an opinion on everything, what do you think about gun control?" I ask, pulling a string of cheese from the pizza and popping it in my mouth.

"Card-carrying member of the NRA," he responds between bites.

"Sheesh, a little extreme, huh?" His passion for firearms originally surprised me, although I guess it shouldn't have since his future plans include the military. Computers and firearms are an intriguing, offbeat combination to me. I'm married to a man who has never been in the same room as a gun.

"Not extreme. We have the right to bear arms. I have the right to protect myself."

"But, truthfully, have you ever actually needed that right other than just to hunt?"

He begins spewing opinions as I stuff myself on pizza. I tune him out for a bit, not really wanting to engage in an in-depth policy debate, but focus back in when he mentions his dad. "Do you know how many times Dad has been accosted by someone on drugs? Or in the middle of some type of adrenaline rush? In theory, a bullet should stop them, but it doesn't always, not under those conditions. That's why I wanted you to try my gun. For your protection, you need enough firepower to actually stop someone. You don't have the experience to understand that a .22 isn't going to do that." His tone dwindles as he picks up a pizza slice. "I want to protect you."

My breath catches. He means that he wants to teach me to protect myself, right? That had to be what he meant. I don't know how to navigate the conversation from here, so I attempt to change the subject. "Ugh," I say, starting to feel the effect of all the pizza, "now I just want to lie down and unbutton my pants."

Tad stops. Actually, more like freezes. What the hell just came out of my mouth?

"Uh, unbutton my pants because I'm so full. I always eat way too much if I skip a meal." I try to clarify my statement. "It would be nice to feel like I could breathe."

He laughs. "That could be arranged."

Oh. My. God. Now I remember why I don't leave the house or talk to people. I should be permanently muzzled.

I make my excuses and beeline across the driveway to home. Ethan and the kids float in the pool. Ethan bobbles up and down on a raft reading his Sports Illustrated while Maya and Zach play Marco Polo around him.

"How did the shooting go?" he asks. "Did you find anything that you want?"

Tad flashes through my mind, but I immediately squelch the thought. "I did," I say, and I tell him about the day and the Walther. I don't mention that I might have found something else I want as well.

PART IV

2009

Chapter 8 ~ January

I pull on a blue sweater and ask Ethan, "Does this look okay?" Not the right question to ask, since he is overly honest.

"I'd change it," he says before he disappears down the steps to watch for his sister, who is babysitting for us tonight. He doesn't understand that reassurance comes in many forms and if I ask, it means I want to look nice for him. He could just as easily say, "You look really hot in the grey one. Why don't you wear it?"

Over the past month or so, I've lost weight. Ethan constantly weighs less than me, albeit not on purpose, and likes to remind me each morning when I watch him step on the scale. No matter how small I am, he always manages to weigh less. It frustrates me, because I don't want to be one of those couples with the stick husband and the beach-ball sized wife. Even when I'm upset with him, I want him to find me attractive and sexy. I want him to be interested in me; the only interest he ever shows is physical and the pressure to live up to that expectation is overwhelming.

If I had a little more will power, I'd make myself bulimic. Then I could eat all the Hershey bars I'd want. But I hate to throw up. Plus I don't see that setting a very good example for Maya. So instead I exercise a lot. My friend Alyssa invited me to participate in a mini-triathlon in Knoxville with her. I thought she was insane. But then I thought about how great it would feel to have a goal to work for. Ethan, of course, encouraged it. I've learned that he will actually put things off to allow me to exercise. It seems to be the one thing he can relate to. He'll bend over backwards and reprioritize if I want to exercise—because he expects me to do the same.

I'm down seventeen pounds. I started out between a size twelve and fourteen. I gained a lot of weight during my pregnancies, but when your youngest kid is over five years old, it is time to admit that it isn't baby weight anymore. Now I fit into my size eight jeans. My goal is to slither into a size six dress this weekend, but eating those damn Hershey bars doesn't help. Ugh. I must control myself and drink more water.

When Ethan asked me on our first date, it shocked me that he was interested because I considered him out of my league. He was this super popular, blond, shorter, muscular athlete, and his confidence impressed me. He competed in every intramural sport. His fraternity dubbed him 'the pride of the house' and it wasn't just because of his athletic prowess. A string of girls followed Ethan around to his games. He graduated before I met him, but still lived in the fraternity house. He had no job, partied every night, slept all morning, and exercised all afternoon. He wore nothing but shredded tees and cut-off denim shorts. He had two tattoos and a couple of earrings. While my friends were mostly proper, uptight engineers, his undergraduate degree was in business. We were complete opposites from the beginning, but somehow that just added to the attraction and we couldn't get enough of each other.

Tonight, I'm searching for a little of that. Tomorrow, Maya and I are taking off for a "bonding" weekend while Ethan stays home with Zach. I hope that our date will provide a connection before we spend two days in separate cities, bolstering us before we divide.

After we're seated at dinner, I attempt to pry Ethan open. "How was your day?"

"Same as always."

"Anything exciting happen? No patients filing lawsuits or quality investigations?"

"I don't want to talk about work, Stella." Ethan's thumb flicks the corner of the plastic menu.

Our waiter appears to take our orders. As he returns to the kitchen, Ethan's twinkling eyes meet mine. "How many beers?"

Here we go. The game. Ethan doesn't want to talk about his day or hear about mine. He wants to know how many beers it would take for me to fuck our waiter. Lovely.

"I don't know," I reply, exasperated. "His adjusted gross income obviously doesn't place him in the eligible bracket."

"Come on, Stella," Ethan cajoles, "play along." That is all Ethan ever wants. Play along.

"Zero," I respond.

"What?"

"You heard me. Sober. Stone cold sober. He may not have any money, but at least he looks me in the eye and asks me what I want. He even offered to help if I need anything. Sober."

That shuts Ethan up. Our dinners arrive and we eat silently. Then we adjourn to a movie, paying a sitter ten dollars an hour for yet another opportunity to ignore each other.

On the drive home, I gaze out the window, remembering college, meeting Ethan, and the chain of events that brought us to this point. I look over at him and ask, "What are you thinking?" By now, I should know that's a loaded question, but on some level I hope that he is examining our relationship or evaluating our evening.

"I was wondering what it would taste like if we made chili and put it on a burrito," he responds. His face is completely straight. This is not a joke. This is his answer.

"Oh." What am I supposed to say to that?

"Why?" he asks. "What are you thinking?"

"Not much. I'm tired." He grabs my hand and we drive the rest of the way home like that. Silent, holding hands. He doesn't understand or relate to the world inside me, no matter how much I want him to. I stopped trying to explain it to him long ago. Numb is the only emotion I feel around him anymore.

After releasing the sitter, our routine resumes. I scrub my face and remove my contacts while Ethan locks up the house. I change into my pajamas while he brushes his teeth. He disappears to find a light bulb to replace the one that fizzled out.

Once I'm snuggled under the covers, Ethan flops on the bed and stares at me, hoping, I assume, that I'll meet his expectation. Instead, I ignore him. Finally, he snakes his arm around me and asks, "Do you want to turn on a movie?"

Shit. I'm tired. I do not want to watch porn. Ethan is trying to bond with me. When we were younger, I was free and uninhibited. I visited strip clubs with him and we rated the girls together, making up back-stories for them as we went. His friends were jealous of my acceptance, but they didn't understand that is wasn't me accepting his faults. It was him accepting mine. Our bond, our connection, was so strong that no naked girl could plant doubt in my mind. He loved me completely, and it freed me. I wanted to be his fantasy. I wanted to explore everything with him, not just his body wrapped underneath the sheets.

His constant pestering smothers me. He pins it all on me, as if I reject him out of spite. He doesn't see me, he doesn't talk to me; he doesn't touch me unless there is an expectation attached. It could be anyone lying here. Ethan wants a warm, uncomplicated body to comfort him, nothing more. "Why don't you sleep with someone else?" I spit the words at him. "Really. Give me a break. I obviously don't meet whatever need you have. Find someone who can."

Ethan pulls back, rolls to his side, and shuts off the light. Under his breath, he mutters, "I don't know how I married you. If I met you now, I wouldn't even date you."

***

The morning shuffle reinforces our distance, and, without a kiss goodbye, Maya and I are on the road. We're going to a concert. I'm going to require an Advil IV to survive this tweenage star. The day is almost tolerable until we check in to our hotel after the show.

Our suite includes a heated pool for her to swim in and a breakfast counter for her to stuff herself on muffins and sugary cereals. It is expensive, but the benefit of separate den and sleeping areas make it worth the money so that she can sleep comfortably while I read. But this concert has her hyped up, and, instead of sleeping, she tantrums.

Maya's almost eight years old, but at times she acts like she's two. I don't understand it. She sleeps with no problem at home, but freaks out when we travel. Why can't that child just lie down and go to bed?

I try to calm her down. I'm afraid someone will call the front desk and complain about the noise if she keeps this up. I talk to her gently and rub her back. She screeches louder, lunging around the bed. If only she would just stop screaming. I want to laugh and tell stories and talk with her, but her uncontrolled energy prevents me from doing so.

I smack her leg. It works; she quiets and curls into a tense ball. I hate hitting her. We try not to spank, especially at her age, but when we've tried everything else, sometimes it seems to be the only thing that will jar her back into reality.

She quietly murmurs, "Mommy, it makes me feel like I don't have any friends when you hit me."

Damn. I don't want her to feel like she has no friends. I just want her to stop screaming.

I explain to her that she does have friends and list all the people who love her. She enjoys that, relaxes, and listens to me drone on and on. Then I finally ask, "Maya, what can we do to help you calm down without a spanking?"

"Hmm," she ponders, "you could probably give me a special treat."

"No, Maya. I'm not giving you special things for misbehaving."

"Humph."

"Is there anything else? A special word or something that would help you remember to calm down when you're feeling out of control?"

"Nope."

"Would you like to call Daddy?"

Maya's eyes widen in excitement as she nods her head in agreement. I dial the phone, hoping Ethan can prevent this storm from recurring. His voice mail picks up. I disconnect the call and shoot him a text requesting that he call me back.

"Where is Daddy?" Maya demands as I place the phone back down on the bedside table.

"He isn't answering right now. Maybe he's reading Zach a story," I say, trying to excuse his absence although Zach has probably been asleep for hours.

"I want Daddy," Maya whines over and over, each repetition sliding me closer to desperation.

Shit. I am tired, and this kid isn't one iota closer to going to bed. Round and round we go with this garbage. Finally, I sigh, "Maya, I can't talk anymore. Mommy is tired and ready to go to sleep."

She tears up and prepares to let loose again. "Please be quiet," I beg. "Let's say prayers." Luckily—for both of us, I think—she agrees. I begin with the rote, "Now I lay me…" and she joins in.

When it comes time to list the things we are thankful for, Maya says, "Thank you God for Daddy. He is my favorite. And please take care of Zach because I miss him. Oh, and Bartles and Jaymes and Squeaky. The end."

No mention of me. Both our cats and even Squeaky, the freaking dead guinea pig, warrant appreciation, but not the mom who just wasted her entire day trying to make a seven- year-old happy.

***

Almost half way home, I ask Maya, "What was your favorite part of the trip?"

"The Fruit Loops," she answers honestly. Of course. Two hundred dollar tickets, a five hour car ride and a hotel suite, but her favorite part cost $3.49 at the grocery.

"What about the concert? Did you like it?"

"Yeah, but it was really loud." She changes the subject. "Do you think Daddy and Zach are reading the comics?" Ethan loves to bury his nose in the newspaper on Sunday mornings, so he barters, offering the comics as a reward to the kids if they don't disrupt him.

"I don't know. Why don't you read one of your books for awhile?" We visited the library last week in preparation for the long ride.

"I don't want to. Are we there yet?" she whines.

"Three more hours, Maya." I sigh, already exasperated.

"But I want Daddy now. I love him best," she proclaims and then proceeds to gush on and on about Ethan, the same guy I have to guilt and beg into spending time with her. I'm tempted to hurl the car into an oncoming semi, but, like the damn responsible person I am, I continue home.

I resent Ethan. I resent how easy it all is for him. I resent how I do all the work for the kids but they love him more because he takes none of the responsibility of raising or caring for them. He's the fun one while I'm always the bad guy. I cook the healthy meals; he hands out the ice cream. I dole out the punishment; he rescues them from time out. I make them hold hands in the parking lot; he takes them to the park with no thought of a little body falling off the top of the monkey bars. I understand that most of that falls into my domain now that I stay at home, but it would be nice if he occasionally at least pretended to be interested in what we're buying our kids for Christmas.

At home, Ethan proceeds to tell me how Zach, my demon child, was a total delight the entire weekend. He didn't have one fit and slept in until ten o'clock this morning. Yesterday he even fell asleep mid-afternoon and

Ethan took a nap. He has been a total joy, which pisses me off because he sure as hell isn't like that around me. Within ten minutes of me walking in the door, Maya stomps off to her room and Zach whines in the corner.

Some days, I think I should leave. My kids would be better off without me. Ethan wouldn't notice anyway, other than the fact he might have to occasionally take a little responsibility. But what would I do? Go find an apartment, a job, and then what? Is a dysfunctional, horrible relationship better than none at all? Do I really want to split my kids so that I have to miss some holidays with them? We'd have less money, the kids would be in daycare, and for the rest of my life it would be my fault. I don't think I can deal with that kind of guilt. Ethan would never, could never, take any of the blame.

If I walk out, I'll be the one at fault. I'll be the one who actually did the leaving, although he has been gone for years.

Chapter 9 ~ July

Ethan wanted to build a giant swing set/tree house monstrosity the moment we moved here four years ago. Up until now, I've held him off by making sure the money wasn't available. I didn't spend it on anything else; I just moved it so that he didn't know it was there. He spends and I save. My job is to balance him out so that we can still afford to take our kids to the doctor when they develop ear infections.

He and the kids checked out a do-it-yourself tree house guide from the library and spent weeks this spring designing what they want. Today, he's circling the wagons to push for it again. He's visiting home improvement stores, plans in hand, and comparing prices for the wood, fasteners, and accessories. I can't get him to repair the bathroom fan, but his enthusiasm abounds when the project is completely unnecessary.

I don't think I'm going to be able to come up with a good excuse this time. Maya and Zach are eight and six now, so it isn't like there's a baby that I have to prevent from falling to its death. The idea of being able to send them to the bottom of the hill to play sounds a little more appealing since I won't have to trek down there and sit in the bugs with them.

The phone rings. Ethan beckons from a home improvement store, salivating over a swing set. "I'm at the hardware store by your tanning salon. You have to come see this predesigned set. It has an option for three swings, a club house underneath, an upper floor with a spyglass and periscope, a slide, a climbing wall, and a row of rings to swing across. It's amazing. And the best part is it's only five hundred dollars."

"This sounds too good to be true," I retort. With as long as we've looked at these suckers, I know a decent one can run easily over a thousand dollars if not two. "Really? It only costs five hundred bucks?"

"You have to come see it. Grab the kids and hop in the car. I'm not leaving until you look at it." Click. He doesn't offer me an option.

The minute I tell them that we are going to inspect a swing set, the kids rush to the van. They chatter all the way to the store and squeal as we walk up to Ethan, who is sporting a broad smile.

"This is it," he announces with pride.

I examine without talking. I'm not upset, but I want to make sure I actually know my opinion before I voice it. If I say anything encouraging and then reconsider, it will result in a giant fight. After I investigate, I have to give him credit. It seems he found a good one, and for an incredible price.

"Okay. I have to admit it looks perfect. If this is the one, let's buy it."

"Really?" He looks surprised. "You don't mind?"

"Nope. You convinced me." With that, I snatch the tag and we round up the kids to check out. Standing in line I ask, "How do you plan to bring this thing home?"

Briefly, Ethan's face goes blank. He hasn't thought that far in advance, but I can see the gerbil running. "We'll use the Newlans' truck, of course. I'll give them a call and see if they're around."

"If you're sure," I say. "This is your project. I'm not volunteering to coordinate a rental to pick it up."

"I'll handle it," he replies. "You won't even have to watch the kids while I build it. They'll want to help."

That seems overly optimistic to me, but I smile and play along. It is nice to see him happy and for once not to have anything to fight about. We pay and somehow, between parting in the parking lot and meeting at home, Ethan talks to a Newlan and confirms that they will help him bring everything home later this evening.

I take the kids inside to cook grilled cheese sandwiches while Ethan goes over to the Newlans' to see who he can rope into driving him back over to the hardware store. I figure he'll be gone a while, so after dinner the kids and I throw on our swimsuits and trek down to the pool for an evening swim. Zach and Maya dive in and entertain each other, so I happily relax in my chair with a book.

An hour or so later, I hear a vehicle pull into our driveway.

"We're home." Ethan beams as he dances through the side gate to the pool, followed by Tad.

"Hey." I look up from my book and jump a little. I didn't realize that Ethan would be with Tad. I figured Theo had been drafted since he's generally the one who does all of the big outside jobs for us. "So what's the plan now, guys?"

"We're going to unload it and lay it all out tonight," Ethan says. "That way tomorrow I can wake up early and assemble it."

"Have fun," I say, dismissing them. They turn around and file back out the gate. I hear the odd curse word and grunt as they move the giant planks down the hill one by one and lay them out. Then silence. It piques my interest. How long can it take to unload a couple of pieces of wood? I'm too curious and have to check it out.

"Kids, please stay in the shallow end for a second," I call to Maya and Zach over my shoulder. I won't walk down the hill, just out the gate. They're both good swimmers, but I don't want them in deep water if I can't see them. I look out. Ethan stoops over his pieces of wood, looking pissed. Tad towers over him, a slightly bored expression on his face. I wonder how much we're going to have to pay him to fix this mess once Ethan destroys it. I bet we'll double the cost of the set overnight.

I hear Ethan mutter, "Shit."

"So are you going to enlighten me?" I yell down to him.

Ethan is obviously fuming as he stomps up to me. I wonder if I should have stayed out of it. "There are no fucking holes. The set was so cheap because we have to measure and drill or bore every single hole to put this thing together. It's going to take all night."

Everything inside me wants to laugh, but I hold it in. I should not delight in his misery, but it is just so damn hard not to. "Sorry about that," I say and manage to keep a straight face. "Are you really planning to do it tonight? Couldn't you just start tomorrow?"

"No." This is going to happen tonight. I can already see it.

"Okay, well, good luck then," I say. "Will you even have enough daylight to finish?"

"Tad can hold a light for me," he grouses.

Perfect, I think. That means I don't have to. "I need to keep an eye on the kids." I know they're fine because I hear them both singing, but I want out of this conversation. Ethan turns, looking dejected, and trudges back down the hill.

When I pack up and bring the kids in from the pool, I see a string of extension cords running beside the deck and all the way down the hill. Tad seems to be helping measure, which makes me feel a little better. Hopefully, his involvement will ensure that the final product will be close to square and won't topple over the first time Maya jumps off a swing.

Once the kids flop in their beds to read for the evening, I meander back down the hill to check on the guys. Both stripped down to just gym shorts and sneakers while I was inside and stream rivers of sweat. I peer down the line of planks; they appear to all have various series of holes and anchors, so I assume the project is close to done.

"Anything I can do to help?" I offer.

"Nope," Ethan responds. "This is about it. One more after this one and we're done. Having Tad here made it go a lot faster."

"Great," I say. "Can I bring you guys anything? Maybe a beer?"

"I don't drink," says Tad. Curious. I don't think I've ever met a college student who didn't drink alcohol. Actually, I believe most of the people with whom I was well acquainted in college only drank alcohol.

"You can meet us by the pool with Gatorade," says Ethan. He turns to Tad, "Want to stay a while and swim to cool off?"

"Sure," replies Tad.

I head back up to the house. Once I'm through the front door, I immediately stop in front of the mirror to examine the swimsuit I've had on since the kids and I went out after dinner. It's cute enough, I guess, but not the super skimpy bikini I would have flaunted in college. My mommy version ties like a bikini, but a small panel grazes my stomach. I check myself from every angle and give a nod of approval. Not perfect, but not unreasonable for someone over thirty with two kids. Wait, why am I doing this? Ethan has seen me in granny swimsuits after having babies. I know he isn't even looking anyway. So why am I completely aware of my appearance? My eyes widen as I realize: because I know *he'll* be looking.

I shake my head and load a serving tray with Gatorades, Pringles, frosted animal cookies, and a beer. The beer and cookies are for me. Maybe they'll help me relax and talk. I throw a couple of extra towels over my shoulder and pick up the cordless iPod speaker. Might as well add some ambiance.

They come through the side gate and cannon ball directly into the pool. Gross. Looks like I'm going to have to super shock with chlorine tonight. Ethan didn't even bother to remove his shoes.

The conversation between them prattles on. I sip my beer and look from Ethan to Tad and back again. They are physically so different. Ethan is a medium sized, muscular, blond athlete; he directly opposes Tad's tall lanky frame topped by dark hair. But both are overachieving, first born males. Both want control of their surroundings and circumstances at all times. Both have trouble relating to their families because they exist on a different level than the people who raised them. Both are strong willed, inflexible, and keep themselves closed off from others.

But the similarities end there. Ethan is a guy's guy. He's popular, friendly, and knows exactly what to say to everyone. Even when he's insulting someone, he makes them feel like he's their best friend. People think they know him because he is so skilled at playing his part, but I know the truth: it's a role he plays. I know the way he really sees them and the judgments he makes underneath his finely controlled veneer. He is intelligent, but he isn't intellectual. Ethan isn't curious about learning or exploring ideas. His interests remain physical, never cerebral. He plays so many sports because he only relates to people physically. Even with me, his interest is purely physical. Otherwise he has nothing to discuss. He focuses on our lifestyle and he wants life to be easy. He doesn't want to think too much. Until me he never voted, but now I badger him into it. He refuses to watch the news. He rarely expresses his opinions. Sometimes I wonder if he has any. He never returns a product to a store or complains at a restaurant even if they completely screw up his order. Ethan does anything to not rock the boat.

Tad, on the other hand, seems more introverted. Like Ethan, I think he plays people, but because he is so intelligent, I get the impression that he likes to see if he can manipulate them. Tad forcefully expresses his opinions — at least, he has any time we've talked — and can debate theories and policies for hours. I don't agree with ninety percent of his views, but spending time around someone who is so openly honest refreshes me and he makes me see the rational points in an opinion I don't agree with. Adulthood hasn't yet trampled him into submission, to that place where he is tentative of expressing himself. He doesn't dilute his argument just to soothe my ego. I guess that's the thing that intrigues me. I understand him because he is just like me.

"Stella. Earth to Stella." Ethan waves his hands in front of my face. Tad floats across the pool on a giant alligator. "I'm going to pick those extension cords up and put the tools away. Can you manage to entertain our guest until I return?"

Ethan walks out the gate and I'm alone, illuminated by only the pool lights, with Tad. "So, are you enjoying your summer?" I search for something to talk about.

He laughs. "I assume that means you didn't listen to a word I said while Ethan and I were talking?"

"Um, not really. Sorry about that." I move over to the side of the pool and sit by the shallow end, dangling my feet in. "I spend too much time around children. It makes for poor conversational skills. At least I'll get a break next week while they're in Vacation Bible School."

"I didn't think you went to church," Tad says, throwing me a quizzical glance.

"We don't. But the bible schools are free and keep the kids occupied, so it's well worth it. The kids learn a moral lesson or two and eat a snack while I receive free childcare. I believe in business, you refer to it as a win-win," I joke.

"Sounds like torture. My parents made me go to church until high school, when I flat out refused. No more. I'm an atheist."

"You believe in nothing whatsoever?"

"Nope," he says. "Life is it. You wouldn't believe some of the stories Dad comes home with. Just watch the news. No God I could believe in would condone this. How can you think otherwise with everything you know?"

Drawing my breath, I consider my response. "I think otherwise because of everything I know. I've grown two people out of thin air. Life, the earth, the skies, they all default to chaos. To me the order imposed, the intricacy of cells, food, and life are the only proof I need. They directly oppose the tendency to chaos. Now, to me that doesn't necessarily indicate a Christian god, especially not one who occasionally answers prayers like they're letters to Santa, but supports the theory of some type of external direction. So we'll have to agree to disagree, because while I don't expect to change your mind, you won't change mine.

"What else do you have planned for the summer, other than pondering the existence of a supreme being?" I ask, changing the topic.

"I'm helping my cousins build a cabin on their property so I spend some days there, but Theo's coordinating that project and I can only tolerate him for so long."

"Yeah, for twins you guys don't seem to have that much in common," I agree. "Well, other than your love of firearms."

He smiles. "If our house ever catches on fire, you'd better evacuate quick. That thing'll go up like a Roman candle with all of our ammunition." Great. That makes me feel a lot safer.

Tad paddles the gator closer to me now. I look down his long, lean body and all of a sudden my stomach flops. I don't hear Ethan moving through the yard anymore. He must be around front arranging everything in the garage.

"Sometimes he talks about you, you know."

"Who?" I ask.

"Theo. Well, Theo and his friends. And I guess I have to throw myself into that category. You are a complete MILF."

Huh? Did he say milk? What the hell does that mean? His face tells me it was a compliment, but I have absolutely no idea how to respond.

"Thanks, I guess. So are you coming back tomorrow?" I try to move the conversation to safer ground. "Did Ethan rope you into helping assemble this mess?"

"I don't think so. I might stop by later in the day to see how it's going, but I'm not waking up at the crack of dawn to work on it."

"Of course not." I chuckle. "I mean, you wouldn't want to drag out of bed before lunch, would you?"

Ethan comes back through the gate. "I'm done," he announces. "You about ready to call it a night?" He looks at me, eyebrow raised.

"Sure."

Tad emerges from the pool and dries off.

"Thanks for giving us a hand," says Ethan. "We'll bring a check to you tomorrow or Sunday."

"Sounds good," replies Tad. He lets himself out and shuts the gate behind him.

Ethan grabs my hand and leads me back up to the house. He must be exhausted, because he doesn't even try to talk me into having sex. He snores seconds after his head hits the pillow. I lie awake beside him, running the evening through my head until I finally doze off.

Saturday morning I wake up to the sound of nothing. Wait. Nothing. My eyes fly open. That never happens. Ethan jostles around beside me or a kid stands at the side of the bed poking my ear asking, "Mommy, are you awake?" as if the answer is not completely obvious.

This morning there is nothing. I don't hear Ethan. I don't hear Zach and Maya clanking breakfast dishes, fighting, or watching television. It should be peaceful, but instead it jolts me completely awake. Where did they all go? I search through the house, but there is no one. I check the garage. Both cars are here. Then I remember.

I look out the back door. It is only seven a.m., but Ethan and the kids must have already been up for at least an hour. Tools and instructions are spread over half of our yard, and the kids sit on a blanket, surrounded by snacks that I assume they consider breakfast, watching with interest. They are all occupied.

I run to the computer, fire up Google, and search for MILF. Mother I'd like to … holy shit.

PART V

2011

Another offer letter arrived today, this one from a small research laboratory. I applied for three separate jobs, all of which I received offer letters from. And all of which I will turn down. Every time I am incredibly angry with Ethan, I apply for jobs with the thought that I will first find employment and then leave him. This time, it was over another poker night.

A little over a month ago, Alyssa invited me to attend a cooking lecture. The thought of getting out of the house for the evening excited me. Even though I reserved my lecture date well in advance on our calendar, some of his buddies invited Ethan to a last minute poker game the same night. He absolutely refused to discuss it. It was my problem. Even when I told him that I felt guilty calling his sister and expecting her to drop everything, he didn't bend. She's *his* sister. Why can't he call her? Oh, right. Because nothing I do matters anyway.

So when I arrived home from the lecture, still fuming, I scanned the classifieds, printed out resumes, and stuck them in the outgoing mail pile.

***

I call his poker group the Divorced Men's Club because only the single and divorced guys attend on a regular basis—other than my husband. That in and of itself doesn't bother me, but Mark, the guy who hosts it, is a real jerk. I hear how he talks about his ex-wife and I saw him in action back when he was still married. None of Ethan's normal, married friends play because Mark is so offensive that they don't want to be around him. In my opinion, by tolerating it, Ethan condones Mark's behavior. Perhaps he feels it justifies his own and then he isn't such a bad guy.

Two nights ago while Ethan was playing poker, Zach woke me up complaining of aching muscles and bad stomach pain. He'd seemed a little weak and tired during his earlier soccer game, not like his usual energetic self, so I wasn't too surprised. I assumed it must be a virus, so I set him up with a pillow and blanket in the bathroom, poured a cup of Gatorade, and wet a washcloth to drape over the back of his neck. Within an hour he was curled into a ball on the bathroom floor, almost unresponsive. His skin seemed off-color. At that point, I decided it was time for intervention. I called Ethan and asked him to come home so that I wouldn't have to wake Maya if Zach required a trip to the pediatric ER an hour away. It is the only time I have ever called and asked him to leave a night out with his friends to help me. He told me he was on his way.

"Where have you been? I called almost four hours ago." I met Ethan at the door a few minutes before two in the morning.

"We were in the middle of a game. I was getting ready to leave, but they were using my chips, and then Mark started describing symptoms he's having and wanted my professional opinion. It's just a virus, Stella. Zach will be okay. With him it's always something."

"You need to see him," I demanded, all but running up the steps to the bathroom. "Feel his forehead. Just look at him."

Zach huddled in the middle of the cold tile floor wrapped in his blanket. Instead of looking pasty and pale, I thought his skin tone had darkened. A lonely plastic duck kept watch from the edge of the bathtub, guarding him.

"Yes, he looks off," Ethan conceded. "But it isn't like he's having a seizure or anything. If you thought it was so important, why didn't you call back?"

I was furious. "Is that our new standard for care? No medical attention until you have a seizure? I didn't call back because I already understood that it was pointless. If you won't come when I call the first time, why would you come if I called again? I'm just overreacting anyway."

I ran the thermometer over Zach's forehead. 103.7. "Mommy," he moaned softly with his eyes closed.

"I know." I kissed his forehead and shot Ethan a glare, daring him to challenge me. Then I carried Zach to the car and floored it out of the driveway.

Turns out my instinct was correct. Zach was close to kidney failure when we arrived at the children's hospital. He was so weak and dizzy he couldn't walk. They admitted him immediately, and, after a few tests, diagnosed him with Addison's disease. When I told Ethan how serious it was, he finally showed concern.

I don't understand how he can be so separate. If the situation were reversed and he had taken Zach to the hospital, I would've been calling every one of Maya's friends, my own friends, and every family member in a two hour radius to find somewhere for Maya to stay so that I could rush to be by his side. I understand that Ethan sees me as a capable adult who doesn't need him, but even if I didn't need him, how could he not see that Zach did? And the truth is I did wish he was there. I was terrified. I knew nothing about the tests they conducted on Zach. I didn't understand the specifics of the clinical trials Zach was encouraged to participate in. Yes, I can read, but I don't have training in those areas and I was asked to make some very important decisions with almost no facts.

And I understand that parents are put into that situation all the time, forced to make the call for their children in emergencies where they may not have all of the necessary information. But Ethan would've understood every word; this is his specialty. However, Ethan didn't deem it important enough to be worth his time to drive up and provide input.

Once the hospital released Zach yesterday evening and he was tucked into his own bed, I packed Ethan's bags and kicked him out of the house.

***

Maya pokes me on the shoulder. "I'm hungry. We didn't have dinner."

Fuck. "Give me a minute," I respond. I didn't sleep at all last night. I assume Ethan rented a hotel room after he left, but I didn't answer, or even read, any of the text messages he sent.

"Can I have an apple?"

"Yes."

She disappears to the kitchen. I scan the room desperately, searching for something to keep me afloat. The Bible that my grandmother gave me as a college graduation gift catches my eye under a pile of mail.

Religion bewilders me, but Ethan and I occasionally visit a church. I think I know God pretty well. Hell, I talk to him all the time. My problem pertains to the reference to sheep. The Christian connotation for sheep is positive, but a friend and I coined the word sheeple back in high school to describe them. They refuse to think for themselves and cling to a herd mentality so that they don't have to consider the implications of their own decisions. Every one of the good Christians I've met judges others against their impossible, and usually changing, standards. When they themselves fall short by cheating on their spouses or committing disability fraud they are magically forgiven. By grace, right? They are complete hypocrites. I want to raise my children with morals, but not with the Christian judgments.

A few weeks ago, they showed a video that really got to me about a father and his handicapped son who run marathons and swim triathlons. The movie repeatedly portrayed the father as the body and the son as the motivation. The father pushed or pulled the son through all of these crazy races and they did it together. I came home and cried for a long time over that one. I look at people like that and it makes me feel so low, like I'm worth nothing. I can't even comfort my kid the middle of the night without being resentful. Here's a guy whose son is crippled and yet he does all of these amazing things for him. It isn't that I don't feel spiritual. I just feel like God must have made a mistake somewhere with me. I mean, how did I attain everything, and somehow end up so empty? How is that even possible? And how could I expect anyone to relate to or feel sorry for me?

Maybe church allows me to think, a little, although I can't voice my opinion out loud unless I want to risk being shunned. It provides me with information to process, evaluate, and discern how it fits in with my life. Our couples class two weeks ago covered 'The Power of Praise' as our topic. It wasn't praise for God, but focused on appreciation for our spouses. Ethan and I hid in the back row as couples volunteered the best compliments and words of encouragement they've received from each other. They listed the character qualities they admire most in their spouses. We had nothing to contribute. Nothing to say. While the others spent their private time praying and praising, Ethan and I negotiated our schedules in whispers; he wanted to squeeze in a long run on the same evening that Maya's dance lessons conflict with Zach's soccer practice.

I detach from him more with every disappointment. Not expecting anything from him is easier and allows me to search for my own balance. That's the whole thing in engineering. Equations must balance or nothing works correctly. So I tweak my raw materials to see what shakes out. If life were an equation, I could solve it. But life is too messy. It doesn't fit in any of my known parameters.

Church and date nights can't save what isn't there. But as I detach, the storm between us quiets and our relationship stabilizes. I search to find myself in this family, this community, this life.

I need balance but this solitude sucks me toward depression. I look at people who are unhappy with their lives and wonder what in hell is wrong with them. They say, if I was only thinner, only had a different job, whatever. Most of them aren't brave enough to make a change that might actually make it better. Most women would do anything to have the lifestyle I do. We live comfortably. We own nice things. Ethan's schedule is enviable. We do all the right things and have all the right superficial friends. No one discusses what happens when you have everything you want.

When I was younger, I would berate my mother for her lack of emotion and simultaneously promise myself that I was always going to act exactly how I felt. Obviously, if I lived that way, I'd be in jail. I've learned to show things appropriately on the outside, even when I want to scream and punch someone. My phone calls to friends slowed down because I don't want to constantly complain about my marriage or children and don't have anything else to talk about.

I don't want to be one of those fruitcake housewives who needs to be medicated to handle her perfect life. I am no wimp. I graduated as Valedictorian, coasted through my engineering degree, and have never,

ever run into anything I couldn't do if I put my mind to it. If I can pass organic chemistry drunk, I should be able to figure this out. What am I missing?

Maya startles me into the present. "Where is Daddy? Did he go to work today?"

"Yes," I lie, glancing over at my phone that is flashing with no less than twenty-three unread text messages. I fabricate an excuse to protect her. "He went to a training class for work. He'll be home soon."

"When?"

"I'm not sure exactly. He wasn't sure how long the class would last." I follow her back up the kitchen. The offer letter glares at me from the counter, demanding attention. If I take the job, Maya won't be able to make her dance classes. She dances every day. My decision would eliminate Zach's option to play traveling soccer if he recovers enough to do so. His practices and games consume our lives. Ethan depends on me being home now. Our established roles balance each other and, if I work, I will be the one throwing everything off kilter. If I want anything for myself, the resulting destruction will be all my fault.

Fighting is pointless now. I must finally accept Ethan for who he is. We are stable. By stable, I mean we don't argue out loud anymore. Not because of a lack of issues, but because it is time for me to accept that my life is what it is. This is the path I chose. Given the chance, with the knowledge I had at the time, I would make the same choices again. I can't blame my unhappiness on any unfortunate event or great tragedy. Some days I still love him for what we had and settle for that. Others, I resent him as much as always.

I shoot Ethan a text without reading anything he has written. "Let me cool off for the night. You can come home tomorrow afternoon."

There is nothing left to argue, only an escape to consider.

Chapter 11 ~ May

"Pay attention. You spend money too fast," I say. Again.

Ethan stares at me and then back at the IKEA website. "But these fit perfectly," he whines. He's picked out a collection of bookshelves, tables, and lamps to decorate the basement.

"It's a basement. The kids roller blade down there in the winter," I argue. "Why do we need a giant room full of furniture now? We just bought that crazy expensive chair for the living room earlier this month."

"Didn't you plan a technology upgrade?" he asks. We're stuck in a technology rut. I resisted a wireless router for as long as possible. It's time for a change. I plan to switch cable/internet companies, buy a new computer and a tablet, and upgrade the router, all at once.

"Um, yeah," I say. "Exactly. We're already making enough changes. Why do we have to do all of it at once?"

"A TV room in the basement gives the kids their own space," he responds. "The cable guys can run the line while they're here."

"But we don't have a TV in the basement."

Ethan looks sheepish. His eyes twinkle and I already know. "You bought a TV?"

He smiles. "It jumped into my cart off the clearance rack at Sam's Club when I went to buy root beer the other day. The kids can watch Netflix with its wireless internet connection. We can just shove them down there and shut the door." He announces this like he expects a giant hug, a high five—and a reward later.

His news momentarily stuns me. Ethan hasn't paid a bill in over five years. The only time he tried to access our bank account for money, they closed our account down for fraud protection because they didn't believe that he was himself. "You bought a TV?" I ask again, because I can't think of anything else to say.

"You have to see it in your head," he says. "We paint the basement. We buy these things from IKEA. We put a couple of old sofas down there with the TV and hook up the karaoke machine. The kids will love it."

I'm speechless. Luckily, a scuffle erupts upstairs to divert me and give me time to think.

"Quit it," Maya yells.

"You're mean," Zach retorts, followed quickly by, "Mommy, Maya hit me."

"Put your shoes on," I holler at them. "We're going outside to release some of that energy."

I turn to Ethan. "I'm taking them outside. Do what you're going to do. Go ahead and put the TV in the basement for now. And write me a list of everything you want to buy and how much it's all going to cost." I stomp up the stairs and pull out my sneakers as the kids zoom to the garage and grab their bikes.

I flop on the front step and pretend to refuel the bikes as they whiz around in circles. I see Ethan out of the corner of my eye, schlepping the TV into the house through the garage so that he doesn't disturb the kids.

A car, minus its muffler, fires loudly. Lovely. Theo from next door is outside working on something. He seems to have no stable job or function.

"Hey, did you hear I got a job at the hospital, too?" Theo yells across the driveway. He shuts off the car and comes over to sit by me. "I wonder if I'll bump into Ethan while I'm there." The eyebrow piercing is gone, perhaps a concession to employment, but a tattoo peeks out from under the neck of his black T-shirt.

"Congratulations. Ethan generally hides in his office with his head down, so you probably won't bump into him without effort or an appointment." I laugh. "What are you doing there?"

"Security," he responds. "I escort people out and stuff. Mostly it's boring. But one guy, he must have been on drugs or something, claimed he had a gun and needed to see his girlfriend. Turns out she was in intensive care because he beat her up. Once we figured out there was no gun, I handcuffed him and kept him until the police showed up."

"Sounds fun." I make a face. "Did you call your dad and warn him you were sending someone his way?"

He sulks. I guess that made his story not so cool. Oops.

"So what are you guys up to?" He changes the subject.

"Ethan is dragging a TV to the basement as we speak. I need to call the cable company and start this whole technology ball rolling, but I keep dragging my feet, mostly because I need a router and have no idea what to buy. Tad knows all that mess. Do you do any of it, too?"

"Nope," he says. "Not at all. But you can just call him."

"Isn't he still at school?" I ask. "And wasn't he going into the military?" I haven't seen him in quite a while.

"Yeah, but he answers his phone," Theo says. "Really, he won't care." He pulls his phone out of his pocket and hands it over. "Here, program his number into your phone."

"All right." I succumb. "Maybe I'll text him instead of calling. That way I won't interrupt anything." Calling the neighbors' kid, who lives nine hours away, out of the blue for advice shrieks of desperation, but I don't know who else to ask.

So I send a text. Short and sweet. "Looking to put in a wireless router at home. Would like your input on what to buy because I have no clue. Can you let me know? Stella"

Splat. Zach's bike flips and he lies on the driveway, bike on top of him, whimpering. I jump up and race to him. "It hurts," he sobs. He extracts his leg for my closer inspection and I notice he's managed to rip a hole in his jeans but just scrape his leg. A bit painful, but I'm pretty sure he'll live. Then he sees the jeans. "Arr! Those are my favorite pants!" He jumps up and takes off into the house, crying. I guess that means nothing's broken.

"Maya, can you pick up the bikes? I need to run inside to check on Zach and help him wash his leg. Good talking to you, Theo," I call over my shoulder. My traumatized kid probably saved me from an hour-long one-sided conversation with Theo about hospital drama. Perhaps I should give Zach a reward.

As I walk through the door, my phone dings in my pocket. "Is now a good time to talk?" Tad texts.

"Sure," I respond. I figure if he has time now, I might as well take advantage of it.

The phone rings. "Hey," I answer. "How's it going?"

"Good. But let me tell you about the router." Tad is all business. "Buy one that is dual-band N," he says.

"Is that a standard?" I inquire. "N? That makes no sense to me. If I ask someone, will they know what I'm talking about?"

"Yes. And make sure it has encryption and some type of firewall. You can also find one with a guest network if you don't want people who are visiting to know your main password."

"Give me a minute," I say. I scurry into the kitchen and scrounge around to find a Post-it note and pen. "Give me that list again."

"N. Encryption. Firewall. Guest network."

"Is there any specific brand? Or type?"

"Just buy one off the shelf. That's about it," he says. "Who's installing this for you?"

"Um, me?" I hear him chuckle.

"Any idea what you're doing?"

"Nope. But how hard can it be? Doesn't it come with a disk or instructions or something?"

"Yes, but they're useless," he says arrogantly. "I take finals next week, but I'll be home by the first week of June. Do you want me to set it up for you?"

"Okay. Sounds like a plan to me," I agree. How can I turn down free installation that I know will work over trying to do it myself, which will most likely result in disaster?

"I'll call you when I'm back in town," he says. "Take care."

"Okay. Good luck on finals."

"See you soon." He hangs up.

Chapter 12 ~ June

A knock at the front door pulls me away from the computer. I throw on a T-shirt over my swimsuit. Having a pool sounded great in theory, but I never considered how much time I'd spend running around my house wearing close to nothing.

I hear a Nickelodeon theme song blasting on the TV in the den as I make my way down to the front door. Tad towers above the doorframe, peering in. Seems like he's grown another six inches since I last saw him. Always tall, now he towers over everything, including my house. He ducks to come in the front door.

"Hey, stranger. You ready to set this thing up for me?"

"Sure," he replies, "but I'm pretty sure you forgot your pants."

Crap. I didn't stop to consider that wearing a bikini with a T-shirt might look like I'm half dressed. Not to mention, Tad's not my neighbors' *kid* anymore. He grew up. Not just literally, being as he's got to be six and a half feet tall, but he is no boy now. He is all man. He seems less awkward, more sure of himself, and exudes a maturity I don't remember from before. I stand half-naked, in my hall, with a man I find very attractive.

"Sorry about that," I mutter. "I actually just had on my swimsuit and threw on a shirt." I try to at least excuse my appearance. "Let me run grab shorts. You can go on down to the computer. It's in the same spot. The router is in the box right next to it." I U-turn and flee back to my room. I thought he said he'd call or something before he showed up. Oh, well. At least it's a convenient time for me, and my router is being installed for free, by someone who actually knows what to do.

By the time I return, Tad has managed to start up my computer, crack my password, and crawl half under the desk with a cable.

"Need any help?"

"You can unpack the rest of the box," he says, not even looking up from his work. "And can you do something about that noise?"

Zach and Maya sit side by side in the floor, watching their show, surrounded by snacks. "Can you guys move up to my room to watch TV for a while?"

No response. Neither one of them even bothers to turn his or her little head to acknowledge that I'm speaking. I walk to the other side of the sofa, grab the remote, and flip off the TV.

"I'll ask one more time, guys. Please move up to my room to watch the rest."

They growl and grumble, but pack up their cheese, crackers, blankets, and pillows, and trudge up the steps.

"Better?"

"Much," Tad says. "Now I can think." He types furiously on my machine. I pull up a chair to watch. I expect some type of explanation. Sort of a here's-what-I'm-doing-now guide so that I can follow the process. But he is completely silent.

Finally, I transplant myself to the sofa to read a book. I figure it will be a while before he finishes the set-up, but I am mistaken.

"Done," he announces.

"Seriously?" That took a grand total of about seven minutes. "Does it connect to everything?"

"No. It works. You asked me to set up the router. Do you need me to do something else?"

"A bit literal, aren't you? When I said set up a router, I meant connect the whole army of technology to it. Just standing alone sending a signal doesn't help much," I counter.

He laughs and his eyes twinkle. "Bring it on." Is he flirting with me? Or have I been stuck around children for so long that I have no idea how to read people?

Over the next couple of hours, we connect the Wii, the basement television that Ethan bought, and a couple of wireless phones and tablets. Finally, it is done. But Tad doesn't leave. He plops in a recliner and seems poised to talk for a while.

"So are you glad to be out of school?" I ask.

"Absolutely," he says. "The only problem is that I'm stuck here. I don't know where I'm going, I don't have a deployment date, and I'm trapped at home until they set it up. So I have way too much time and nothing to do. But I can't get a job or do anything productive because they could call me at any moment."

"That kinda sucks. I'm sure Ethan can find plenty of odd jobs around here if you're interested. There is always a list of stuff to do that we don't have time for. We should probably prioritize it, but we prioritize our free time instead."

"Like what?" he asks.

"I'm pretty sure there's a tree in the backyard that needs to come down. And we keep talking about adding a couple of outlets in the basement and switching the wiring around, but I only know enough to blow something up."

"I'd be happy to help," he says. "At school, I always helped people on projects. But then it got to where they asked me all the time and wanted me to do their work. So I planted bugs and wrong answers in the programs to see if they'd catch them."

"Are you telling me that you're going to burn down my house to see if I'll notice you incorrectly wiring my basement?" I tease.

His eyes meet mine. "Not the same," he says. I can't read his expression. "Just making conversation."

"You'd better not hack into my router for anything illegal. If I learn you're conducting a cyber war from my IP address, I'll be pissed."

"Cyber warfare." Tad audibly huffs. "What exactly do you think you know about cyber warfare?"

"I know what I read in Newsweek, which probably means I know significantly less than you do. Care to enlighten me?"

Tad's face beams as he begins a sermon on the dangers of regulating cyber warfare. I don't agree with many of his opinions, but he meets each of my points with a counterpoint as his gaze directly challenges mine.

Our words are benign, but butterflies flutter in my stomach. I break eye contact to mute the intensity. "Do you ever have a superficial conversation?"

"Nope. I only talk when I have something to say." He pauses, then adds, "Or someone I want to talk to."

I'm silent in response. Was that supposed to be a joke?

He smiles again, but it isn't casual. "So, did you ever buy that Walther?" he inquires, a vulture hovering before he descends.

"Yep. It's locked upstairs in my closet."

"How often do you shoot?"

"Uh, just that once." I'm embarrassed to admit that I purchased the gun but haven't fired it. Ethan doesn't shoot. I don't have anyone to accompany me. "I've never actually used it."

"You should shoot with me again," he issues the invitation confidently. "Maybe next weekend?"

Tad's arms around me, his chest pressed against my back, memories flash through my mind and I shove them away. "Ethan mentioned he'd like to learn since we have the gun in the house now. Could he come along?" The words erupt from my mouth, forming a wall between us before I consider the offer. Not alone. Not alone with Tad. "I'll mention it to him."

The garage door opener kicks in, cutting off any response. "Ethan's home," I say. "Want to show off your accomplishments?" Saved by the garage. And my husband.

Ethan walks in, covered in sweat, wearing nothing but a pair of basketball shorts and running shoes.

"Just ran about fifteen miles. I'm moving faster." He smiles and kisses me on the cheek.

I have to wipe it off due to all the sweat. Yuck. "Want to see your new technology in action?"

"Absolutely." He kicks off his shoes. "Hey, Tad. Thanks for helping us out. You know if Stella tried it, the whole thing would implode."

"No problem," Tad says, "but I have to leave it to her to show it off. I didn't realize how late it is. We're going to my grandparents' house for dinner, so I've got to bolt." He pauses at the door and adds, "Give me a call if you have any problems with it, Stella."

Ethan pulls me to him. "I missed you today," he says and then he kisses me. I melt into his arms, trying to appreciate what I have, even though he drips on me and it's disgusting. I kiss him back harder, trying to block thoughts of Tad.

Chapter 13 ~ August

This happens every blasted storm. I think the electrical grid in our town must have been built in the 1920s. Every time it rains hard or long, we lose power. The electric company earned a speed dial number on my phone. I figure the squeaky wheel gets the oil, so the minute that power goes down, I squeak.

It started last night around midnight. I always wake up when the power goes out because the nightlights quit and the white noise clocks and fans shut off. We run fans and noise clocks in all of the bedrooms. Excessive precautions perhaps, but the music booming from the cars next made them necessary. Especially Theo's. I was so excited when he left for college, thinking I'd escaped that booming bass. Then he dropped out and moved back home. Now I'm stuck with it again, night after night, his mating call to the world.

While Ethan snored, I ran around, positioning pushbutton lights in all the bathrooms so the kids could see to walk to the toilet, and then distributing our phones and tablets with white noise in every room. Thank goodness for that app.

As I retrieved my phone from the charger, a text message from Tad flashed. "Power's out. Let me know if you need anything." I wanted to respond and inquire as to what type of late night help services he was offering, but instead I called the electric company, sat on hold, punched in the number three to report an outage, and left a callback number for them to reach me with an estimated time that the power might be back on.

Fortunately, everything is back on this morning, the noise apps did their duty, and all is good until the kids decide they wanted to stream a movie. We have no internet connection. So I guess it is time to call Tad. Again. This is probably the fourth time I've paged him to help me reset the router and hook everything back up in the past few months.

Tad and I are friends. I enjoy talking to him when he visits, but I feel guilty paging him over and over to help me with silly problems like this. Well, maybe not too much so, because it gives me an excuse to talk to him, but I don't want our friendship to be based on him doing chores for me. We flirt and banter a bit, and I relax when we talk and hang out. Most of the time, no one sees me just as me. I'm identified as Ethan's wife. Or as Maya or Zach's mom. But no one in this town knows me for the person I truly am. They didn't know me during college, when I worked, or before being politically correct for Ethan's job dictated the opinions I'm allowed to express. With Tad, the pressure releases and I can be myself.

"You available?" I text. I don't even bother to sign my name anymore. He knows who it's from. Twenty seconds later, my phone dings.

"Yep, just for you," he responds. I don't have to wait three minutes before he knocks at the door.

"What can I do for you this time?"

"Same as always," I tell him. "My router requires your service."

He smiles and plods down the stairs. I pull up a chair. As he types, we talk.

"You hear anything about when you're leaving yet?"

"Not for a while," he says. "They still haven't even figured out where I'm going. I call every week and push them, but I don't have a straight answer."

"Sucks to be you." I laugh.

"It does." He turns from the keyboard and looks at me. All of a sudden, I realize what I'm doing. It was so unconscious that I didn't even notice. My chair is right next to his and I've reclined into him with my feet propped up on my desk. Perhaps a bit too casual. And a bit too close.

"Sorry," I say, pulling my feet back down under me to sit up straight in the chair. This line confuses me. Before, Tad intrigued me, but he was just my neighbors' kid. Now, he's an attractive man who perhaps I'm a little too comfortable around. But it is hard to put up that wall. I've known him for so long that I just automatically relax in his presence.

He looks at me again. Not just a glance, but *that* look, the one that kicks me in the stomach. "You know what my mom thinks, right?" he asks.

"Huh?" I don't really know Tad's mom. We were introduced back when Ethan and I first moved here, but we never developed a relationship. She scurries from the car to the house and nods my way occasionally in acknowledgement, leaving me with the impression that she is insanely busy. I can't imagine she thinks about me at all.

"Well," he leads into it, "she asked me why I spend so much time over here. She asked about your intentions."

My intentions? My mind spins. My intention is for you to fix my router and teach me to keep it functional so that I don't require your assistance every twenty minutes. That is my intention. I have a husband and kids. While I'm flattered, she can't seriously think that I'd pursue her son. Could she?

I guess I'm silent long enough that he feels the need to continue.

"It isn't so unthinkable, is it?" he asks. "I mean, Theo's friend Matt thinks you're unbelievable. Remember when he was taking care of our plants while we were traveling and he borrowed your garden hose? You were all he could talk about for weeks. And we have a lot in common."

Holy shit. How do I respond to that? I'm thirty-six years old. And married. With children. I did say married, right?

"Wow," I finally sputter. "I'm flattered."

"You should be," he says.

"So what does she think about the girls you date?" Maybe he can tell me stories of the girls he dated in college. I want to move this conversation toward a neutral topic.

"I don't."

"You don't date, or you don't want to tell me about it? Or your mom doesn't know about them?"

"Pretty much all of the above. I'm good friends with lots of girls, but I've never had a relationship. I'm too busy."

"So what, you just party, sleep around, and leave them the next day?" I joke.

"Nope, haven't made it to that part yet," he says.

"Not at all?"

"Nope."

"Don't you want to?" This is more and more curious. What kind of twenty-three-year-old guy has not had sex? Or wanted to?

"At some point," he says, looking back at the computer. "It just isn't a priority right now."

"All righty, then." I sigh. "I guess we've about exhausted that subject. So can you actually spend some time and teach me how to fix this blasted router myself in case they call you up and you're gone in a week?"

His eyes flash and he's back to business. And when he's business, he's all business. But when he actually lets down his guard enough to show a bit of himself, a personal bit, he's a completely different person. One who is, I think, damaged, scared, and tries to let people in but can't quite trust enough to let go. I can see it in his eyes.

He spends the next hour walking me through how to use my IP address to access my router, explaining what the different fields do, and teaching me how to reset it, but our conversation doesn't cross the line again. He holds me at a distance, as if he peeked through a door and what he saw outside scared him.

***

Ethan walks in the door after work and immediately says, "Tad was here," as he smiles and kisses me.

"How do you know that?"

"The kids are quiet." He laughs. "That must mean our router is working."

He pulls me to him, wraps his arms around me, and kisses me. I love this part of the day on the occasions when we're actually getting along.

He comes in, we steal a moment before we're bombarded with the kids and life, and he holds me like he used to. Like he did back when I was the world to him, before the world got in the way. His eyes smile as he pulls back, leaving his arms around my waist.

"You realize you have a boyfriend, right?" he teases.

"Not quite." I say, maybe a little too fast. "What I have is a kid next door who keeps our house running."

"Tad is completely into you. He dashes over here every time you call. Just watch. If I send him a text or give him a call, he will *not* be at our door in thirty seconds."

"No, he isn't. He's just bored. He's stuck at home, has nothing else to do, and probably figures if he hangs out here long enough, we'll employ him. Maybe he's smitten with our checkbook."

"Maybe," Ethan kisses my face intermittently as he talks. "Let's try it out."

"Try what out?" I clasp my hands behind his neck to control their trembling.

"I'll call him. We still need that electrical work done in the basement. Let's see how long it takes him to respond to me instead of you." Ethan reaches down into his briefcase, searching for his cell. He places the call, and it goes to voice mail. "Tad, give me a call when you have a chance. I want to see if you have time to come do a job for us," he says, then hangs up.

Let the games begin.

Chapter 14 ~ September

After Ethan left the voice mail message, I spent a while convincing him that it would be smarter to bring in an electrical contractor. The contractors offered to upgrade our panel at the same time, and there was less risk of error, not to mention liability insurance if something did go drastically wrong. So while Ethan was working, I scheduled several companies to quote the job. All of them wanted a minimum of five hundred dollars. And all of them wanted to rip holes in walls and floors and completely destroy the house.

So finally I caved in. I told Ethan to hire Tad, with the caveat that I would not be involved. Even though I have an engineering background, and even after the experience with Ethan building that awful wall that came in at triple the budget and four times the labor, I decided to sit this one out. I needed to remove myself from the equation.

The last month hasn't been easy. When I see Tad, he always stops to chat. He invites me, or both Ethan and me, to shoot with him almost every weekend. I considered it. We even booked a babysitter more than once. The first time, she cancelled, which gave me an easy out. The second time, I cancelled, but told Ethan that she bailed again. It isn't that I don't want to go. If anything, I want to go more than I should. He confuses me. I don't know if he intentionally baits me or not, but I do know he makes me think and feel things that I shouldn't, so the easiest thing to do is avoid him completely and pray that he'll be stationed and leave soon.

Only one person knocks on my door at nine a.m. As soon as I hear it, I know it's time for me to suck it up and get it over with. Tad ducks in, smiles, and says, "Lead the way."

Ethan warned me this morning that Tad would be stopping by to check everything out, measure, and gather supplies so they can start work on Saturday. Actually, I believe his exact words were, "I invited your boyfriend over for you this morning. Keep an eye out for him." I apparently wasn't clear enough when I told him I didn't want to be alone in the house with Tad.

"Follow me," I say and lead the way down to the basement. I explain the changes we want, show him locations where we want to drop outlets, and draw out how we want to rewire the lights. Then I take him to the electrical box in the bathroom and pivot toward the stairs, intending to leave him to examine and measure.

"Wait," he says. "Hold this for me." He dangles a measuring tape. So I help him measure, which sends us back down to the basement. "It would be helpful if you had the house plans so we could see the wiring schematic," he says.

"Right here." I turn to a cupboard and pull them out. They are ancient blueprints, but still legible enough to read. We spread them across the floor and sprawl down to examine them. He is close. So close that I can smell him. I can't concentrate, although I have plenty of experience reading a blueprint.

"So I thought about what you said before," he confesses, flipping through the prints and running his finger along the lines as he deciphers them.

Uh-oh. "What I said about what?" I think the topic just shifted away from electrical outlets.

"From our conversation a while back," he answers, picking up a thread I don't yet grasp. "A girl. I'm traveling back to St. Louis to attend homecoming and visit a friend. I invited a girl."

"You did, huh? Good for you." I congratulate him.

"I'm driving there next weekend and we're staying in a hotel," he continues.

"You do know what she might expect, don't you? Or have you had that discussion? You might want to prepare yourself just in case."

He gives me a sheepish grin. "Yeah, I thought of that."

We finish reviewing the prints and he packs up to go. Thank God. "Tell Ethan I'll be back on Saturday to start work."

"Will do," I say. And he is gone.

***

When the weekend rolls around, Ethan and Tad lock themselves in the basement for hours. I hear hammering, drilling, and who knows what else, but I'm not down there, so it's all good with me. When they're done, we have exactly what we want. The lights work. The outlets work. We are no longer dependent on extension cords winding through the damp corners of the floor. I should have known. Everything Tad does works perfectly.

It isn't until the following Saturday afternoon, coming home from the grocery store and pulling into the driveway, that I notice the empty driveway next door. Right. Tad's Corolla is missing. He is going to St. Louis with that girl. My stomach plummets.

What in hell is wrong with me? Am I seriously scoping out the neighbors' driveway to check to see if their son is home? But the more I think about it, the more I realize that I do it all the time. Actually, every time I pull in I instinctively look over to see if he is there or not.

Enough. I put the van in park, shut it off, and exhale hard, trying to push the thought out of my mind. Time to take in the groceries.

I successfully block it all out until the middle of the week, when Tad and I both pull into our driveways at the same time. He jumps out and races across the lawn to talk. A giant smile spreads across his face.

"Good weekend?" I ask, trying not to make too much eye contact. Just act normal, I tell myself. God, I suck at normal.

He doesn't even have to answer; the glee radiates from his face. I haven't heard the story, don't know the girl, and already know what happened. "It was great," he says. "I'll come over and tell you about it."

"How about one day next week?" I stall. "The kids are preparing to start school and I'm juggling pencil boxes, paper, and binders out the wazoo."

"Works for me." With a wink, he continues, "Thanks again for the talk. You did this," and walks away.

I did this. Did I? I search through my mind over and over as I load my milk, water, and protein bars into the house.

Chapter 15 ~ October

The week turns into a few weeks. Settling the kids into the first month of a new school year and coordinating schedules always takes way too much time. Meeting teachers, learning how to handle assignments, and registering the kids for all of their extracurricular activities occupy my mind and my time, which is good, because it distracts me from an unsettling storm of emotion that tries to creep in. With my thoughts occupied, I shove Tad away. Or I try to, until he materializes to tell me about his weekend in St. Louis.

The morning knock at my door isn't surprising. Tad strolls in and flops down on the sofa to talk.

"Make yourself at home, why don't you?" I whack him playfully on the shin before settling into a chair across the room.

"Will do," he replies with a grin. "Did you make me breakfast?"

"Men. Why is it all about what a woman can do for you?"

"It isn't," he responds, then emphasizes, "Well, not always."

"Sure. Maybe I should ask your mom about that. Or perhaps your girlfriend. I assume you've ensnared some unsuspecting girl by now."

"Not quite." Tad pauses and shakes his head. "But I did take that girl to homecoming."

"So tell me all about it," I say, not so much because I want to hear, but because this is obviously the reason for his visit.

"It was really fun," he starts. "We drove up on Friday. Talked the whole way—"

"Oh," I interrupt, "is she from here? I assumed you knew her from school."

"No, she grew up here. Some mutual friends introduced us this summer. She invited me over to watch movies a few times, snuggled up, and then always seemed expectant and confused when I left in the evening once the movie ended."

"Seriously?" This guy perplexes the hell out of me. "So she apparently hit on you and wanted you to kiss her or make a move, and, instead, you went home?"

"Yes. She didn't tell me she wanted anything else. I don't guess at people's intentions. I expect them to tell me."

"And this is the same girl you took to St. Louis, right?"

"Yes."

So this girl shows interest in him. She invites him over, makes passes at him, and, if I assume correctly, is now sleeping with him. If he has a girlfriend, then he certainly doesn't feel anything for me.

"Sorry. Keep going with your story."

"Anyway, so the day we were there, she annoyed me. I sat for hours waiting for her to finish her hair and nails. It took forever. Then we had dinner with my friend and his wife, watched the game, and went to a club."

"You drink now?" I inquire, surprised.

"I drove."

Of course. I should have guessed as much. "Do you dance?" I ask, raising an eyebrow. "I mean, is it weird to tower over people on the dance floor?"

"Nope. I don't dance," he says. "But I stood still and she danced around me, which was pretty entertaining. Then we went back to the room." His eyes drop; he won't look at me.

"And had sex?" I fill in. "If you can't say it, then you probably shouldn't do it." I have to make this into no big deal, I tell myself.

"Well, yeah," he grins sheepishly.

"So are you glad you did? Are you guys, like, a thing now?" I need to remember this is good. I should be happy he found someone. It is time to release this nonsense and stop misreading the situation as something completely inappropriate and probably completely in my head.

He shrugs his shoulders. "It was okay, but I don't understand what everyone's all excited about." His eyes twinkle when he says it, so I can't discern if he's being sarcastic or not.

"Are you serious? Did you not enjoy yourself?"

"It took a really long time. Like two hours," he gloats.

I think he's bragging because he lasted so long. I barely manage to keep a straight face. "Then she evidently had no idea what she was doing. If you ever described me as two hours of underwhelming, I'd have to hunt you down and kill you," I retort. Crap. Did I just say that out loud? My mouth speaks before my brain thinks sometimes.

His eyes flicker and hold mine for a moment. The connection dissipates as quickly as it formed and he tells me about the rest of the weekend before he moves along to his news. "Guess what?" His face animates with excitement. "The call finally came. I'm moving to Monterey, California, the first week of December."

"Congratulations. You said you wanted to be as far away as possible. It sounds like you finally got your wish."

He delves into the details of moving and military stuff, half of which I don't understand, while I nod my head and listen. The first of December is a month and a half away. The thought pushes the air out of my chest.

"So you're not staying for Christmas?" I interrupt him. "Won't your parents be crushed?"

"I don't care. I requested to leave before Christmas so that I don't have to deal with all of that family mess."

We talk for a little while longer and then I close the door behind him. When he is out of sight, I sink to the floor and sit, back to the door, staring at the ceiling. When I don't see him, I'm fine.

I love Ethan, even if I hate him and a distance gapes between us. I love Maya and Zach. So why is it that when Tad walks through that door and looks into my eyes, I forget all that? Why do I feel like I would follow him to the ends of the earth just to have a conversation with him?

Six weeks. I will fight and survive it six more weeks. I was fine until June, when he came home and threw me completely off kilter. Even since then, my self-control hasn't wavered. I maintain a friendly distance without crossing those lines. I am faithful to my husband and my family and I swear to myself at this moment that I always will be. I will not risk my marriage, my children's stability, or my own future on another man. Ethan trusts me, I tell myself, and he is too good, too pure to disappoint. I will not violate that trust and crush him along with everything we have built.

Chapter 16 ~ November

My friend Heather plans to visit this weekend. I met her my senior year in college. Ethan and I were already together by then, but she and I became close friends. Then we graduated, I married, and we started our jobs. She became a little too possessive of my time. She called every day, back in the days before cell phones, sometimes multiple times. Guilt creeps in when I look back now, since I cut her completely out of my life. But our marriage was new. The transition to living together stressed our relationship and I couldn't handle a friend whose expectations put constant pressure on me.

One day she called four times before I arrived home from work. At that point, I worked twelve hour days with an hour commute either direction. The transition from student with no responsibilities one week to married career woman the next overwhelmed me. Generally exhausted and unthrilled with my job, I'd arrived home a little later than normal because I stopped on the way for groceries.

The first message contained a happy, "Give me a call when you get in." By the time I listened to number four she was both angry that I hadn't called and worried that something happened to me. It was all a bit extreme since I was later than usual by only forty-five minutes. Ethan hadn't even noticed that I wasn't home yet.

She tied herself to me and it confined me, like she was trying to intrude on my relationship with him. So I pulled away. I value my independence; allowing myself to be vulnerable and consistent with one person is difficult for me. I chose Ethan. I didn't speak to her for over ten years.

Then social networking arrived on the scene. I resisted, but registered as a way to escape the house when I couldn't physically leave. Ethan hated the idea. He didn't understand why I would bother to reconnect with people who didn't care enough to call. At first I felt the same way, but soon I realized that the same people I talk to in real life maintain better contact with social media, not to mention our extended family loves seeing pictures of our kids. It provides me with a way to keep up with people I otherwise couldn't due to schedules or distance. And, of course, I reconnected with Heather.

Our interactions started as small comments on posts, just light conversation. Then it progressed to longer personal emails and phone calls. Heather gives me the impression that she's jealous of me, which is ironic because she ended up with the life I wanted. She travels constantly for her contract engineering job. She tells enviable tales of trips to Paris and Japan, relocations for projects, and fascinating assignments she's involved in. I guess we swapped destinies, because in college she told me she wanted to marry a nicely built blond guy and cart a few tow-headed children around.

During our short stints as friends, she has never had a boyfriend. She tells perplexing stories about her past relationships, which range from entertaining to restraining-order-worthy. Her eccentric passion focuses on random things, such as specifying the type of rubber a clown nose should be made from. History overflows in her stories of elaborate cotillions, giant hoop skirts, and sordid origins from her father's supposed ties with the mafia. She was raised in northern Minnesota, so most of the stories seem a little out of place.

I bounce around the house, planning entertainment for our weekend visit. I didn't clean until today because otherwise Maya and Zach will destroy it and it will look like I never bothered to clean at all.

I walk into the kids' bathroom to check out their bathmats and scrub all of the dry toothpaste out of the sink. As I flip on the light, I hit the fan switch by mistake. A horrible screech and cough follow, then a loud buzzing sound.

That fan is a giant pain in the rear. It hasn't functioned correctly since we moved in, but there are always bigger problems to worry about. And the kids were so small that their tiny baths never required a fan.

But now Maya is growing up. She takes long hot showers and steams up the entire room. Perhaps it is time for a new fan. I check the clock. I have at least five hours until I have to retrieve the kids from school. That should be plenty of time. So I hop into the car and cruise through four home improvement stores until I find a fan/light combination that is the right dimension to cover the hole that'll be in the ceiling when I remove the old fan.

Once I arrive home, I set everything out in Maya's room, page through the instructions, and realize I have to figure out how to pull the old fan down. Hmm. How hard can it be? I shut off the breaker box and dig a tiny head flashlight our of Maya's drawer so that I can see in the bathroom. My dad gave the kids head flashlights as a joke, but those suckers are handy—as long as no one sees me; I look like I'm ready to go spelunking.

I undo a couple of screws and the plastic grille comes down pretty easily, along with a snowstorm of insulation. I forgot about all that blown insulation in the attic. So I grab a pair of goggles from the garage and continue. I don't see anything holding this thing in the ceiling. So I pull. And I pull some more. Finally, hanging above the toilet, clutching the fan housing, I realize this may be a losing battle. What am I supposed to do now? Ethan is not going to be thrilled if he arrives home from work to this mess.

I lower myself back down to think. I can't. But I don't have any other options. I look out the window and Tad's Corolla sits in the driveway. So I shoot him a text. "You busy? Interested in installing a bathroom fan?"

Three minutes later, he responds, "Sure, when?"

Ha. "Now?"

No response appears. After a few minutes, just when I decide he isn't going to answer, a quick knock announces his arrival.

"At your service," he calls as he lets himself in. "You realize I got out of bed for this."

Oh, to be twenty-three again. I can't remember the last time I slept in past seven. "Up here," I yell and he hops up the steps to Maya's bright pink room.

"What a mess." He gawks. "What exactly do you expect me to do?"

I pass a mirror along the way to Maya's room. Shit. My tank top and gym pants might qualify as acceptable if insulation didn't cling to every square inch of my body. Tiny gray puffs adhere to my hair. And I never stopped to take off my spelunking light or goggles. The queen of sexy, that's me.

Tad looks me over and laughs. "Nice outfit."

"Thanks, Captain Obvious," I respond. "Time to install my fan."

Tad gathers a few more tools and a ladder. "Someone needs to climb into the attic," he says. Luckily, an access point is located in the top of Maya's closet, not ten feet away. Unluckily, it takes a contortionist to climb through because the cut-out in the ceiling is only about two square feet. And someone installed it above a shelf. Designed by a genius.

My gaze shifts from Tad to the hole and back again. "I've never been up there. Ethan is part monkey and he pulls himself up with his upper body. How exactly do you think this is going to happen?"

"I'll make it up," he boasts with total confidence. "Hold the ladder." We clear a spot in Maya's closet and finagle the ladder as close as possible. I stand to the side to stabilize it as he climbs. We're so close that the current running between us electrifies the air.

I guess sometimes being a giant is beneficial because standing on the top of the ladder he is almost able to sit on the beam above us. Huh. He swings his legs up and ten seconds later yells, "Grab the housing, quick."

I hop on top of the toilet and snatch it just in time before it falls. All right. Step number one complete. Now a giant hole gapes in my bathroom ceiling.

I pluck the new housing from a pile of insulation and, after measuring, we realize it is going to need some extra work. "I'm coming back down," he says, so I step back into the closet to stabilize the ladder again.

His feet come down first and he bends in some strange way to emerge. Holy crap. I'm standing right in front of, well, his mid-section. I can't help but peek. The gym shorts he wears outline the obvious.

In the next instant, he stands in front of me. We're alone in a closet, which brings back every sixth grade fantasy playing seven minutes in heaven I ever had. The connection holds and we stare intently at each other. I catch my breath, look away, and the moment passes. "Let's work on that fan," he says.

So we finish it up, which takes longer than I thought it would. The entire time, blood tingles from my fingers to my toes. I second-guess every movement I make, no matter how small, and suddenly realize that I'm trying to impress him. I wince. That's me, impressing guys half my age while covered in insulation. I married Ethan for a reason. I can't fathom trying to tame another one.

But maybe that's the point. Tad is untamed. Ethan and I have been together for so long that being with him is almost like being with myself, at least when we're getting along, which isn't much these days. I know his every move. When he touches me, he knows my body as well as I do. He plays me like a well practiced piece on the piano, perfectly but with no challenge. The routine comforts me, knowing where things are going at all times, but the tingle is gone. I can't remember the last time he looked into my eyes and made me want to melt through the floor. Tad's look contains more fire than the orgasm that Ethan gives me faithfully almost every night.

Chapter 17 ~ November

"He did what?" I ask Heather again. This is our last private time, crowded into a tiny table in front of the pizza place in the food court. We drove separately to the mall since it puts her forty-five minutes closer to home. I've spent our shopping hours wrestling internally. Can I confide in her? Since she lives hours away, she is removed from my daily life. We share no mutual friends. I don't have to worry that she will gossip or wonder who she might tell. But I don't know if I can admit it to her. I can barely admit the truth to myself.

"He asked me to sleep with him. We were both assigned to the same project in San Francisco. Every time I left my hotel, he conveniently finished with whatever distraction he feigned in the lobby and followed me. I spent the entire project avoiding him."

"And he was married?" I choke.

"Yes. It disgusts me. I saved all the text messages and emails he sent me. I'm still considering forwarding them to his wife. What kind of asshole would do that? His wife is sitting at home with their children."

"But you don't know anything about their relationship. He's probably lonely if he travels all the time. I don't understand why it makes you so angry. It isn't like you caught the guy cheating on you. You turned him down. So why ruin his life? Just move along." I think I'd be flattered if someone offered to cheat on their spouse with me, even if I had no interest at all. I guess my self-esteem is more dependent on feeling attractive than hers is. I'll take anything as a compliment.

"But she deserves to know." Heather's cheeks flush. Panic and relief flood me simultaneously. Thank God I didn't tell her.

"What if she doesn't want to?" I can't help myself. I want her to comprehend the other side. "What if he has tried to communicate with her for years and she doesn't understand? What if all of the signs dance in front of her and she refuses to see them? What if she has actively chosen to ignore them to preserve her façade because that's where she wants to remain?"

"It doesn't matter. She still deserves to know."

"What if it was a one-time thing? What if his attempt to connect with you was the only time? What if it sent him reeling and he realized he made a mistake? You could destroy his entire life over a few conversations. You could destroy a family with children. Nothing even happened between you. If you owe it to her, then do you owe it to him to know the whole truth and not just the part that offends you?" I twist my engagement ring underneath the table.

"That's his problem. He shouldn't have done it. I live my life open and honestly. I guess it's too much to expect other people to do the same. It isn't my job to protect him."

She hasn't been married. I have. For thirteen years. Ethan and I have been constant companions for better and worse and all that good stuff. She doesn't understand the lifetime of hurt that builds up. Yes, there are good times and, yes, we love each other. But some hurts run too deep; they are almost impossible to forget or move on from. And, over time, those accumulate to a point where for every fight, every small infraction, a list of grievances pile up that span years. After a while, the arguments fade away; they don't take place in words anymore, because you know each other so well you don't need to have the fight. All that endures is the silence. You are surrounded by the noise of everyday life, of children fighting, dinners being made, homework being done, and life going on, but underneath looms a deep profound silence where you realize you are alone. You accept that the spouse that you pinned all of your hopes and dreams on isn't capable of fulfilling them. I have no idea how to convey that to someone who isn't married.

Heather and I finish our lunch, pick up our bags, and walk toward the parking garage. I can't believe I almost trusted her. I planned to tell her. I crave a sounding board to talk myself out of what may be the worst decision of my life. But that door is bolted shut. No matter how far removed she may be from my daily life, I know who she'll tell.

I orbit the idea of Tad in my head. I try to un-stick it, but I can't. He leaves in less than three weeks. I thought I could control and manage my emotions, but now I'm relatively certain I can't. How do I initiate this? Do I want to? What exactly would I do? Do I trust him enough? Will he react the same way Heather did?

We say our goodbyes, but I remain in my car in the parking lot, shaking. Sometimes I think I love Tad. On some level I must or I would never consider this. I love that he penetrates the shell that surrounds me, and that he understands an intellectual part of me that almost no one else comprehends. I love the chemistry and connection between us that feels like a flame licking at my insides. I love feeling young and carefree again; with him there are no health care invoices, bills, or budgets to discuss. I love that being close to him is something that is mine alone and I don't have to share it with Ethan or the kids. I love the fact that nothing between us has to stand up to the harsh daylight of reality.

But fear and anxiety swirl through my mind. I shudder to consider the ramifications on my marriage. I trust him to be discreet, but the assumption that he'll admit his feelings could make my entire marriage blow up in my face. I don't want him to think I'm propositioning him for sex. Am I really willing to risk my entire life for this conversation?

I think I am.

Maybe it's a mid-life crisis, but I'm growing older. Heather and I stopped for a few drinks one night while she was here, and perhaps it's vain, but when I walk into a bar, I expect to be noticed. Men still look me over, but it isn't the same crowd anymore. I smile in the mirror and watch the lines around my eyes deepen with each passing month. My grey hairs increase exponentially every time the kids argue. My heart sinks further every time Ethan and I turn out the light in silence.

What if this is my last chance to feel this way? I'm amazed that my body can still respond like this to the physical presence of a man I've never actually touched. It reminds me that I'm still alive. Sometime way back in history I felt like this about Ethan, but, honestly, I can't remember when.

Like so few people in this world, Tad recognizes the loneliness condensed beneath my skin because it reflects his own. In those hours when our lives collide, the fact that I can forget my solitude even a moment is everything.

Some people cheat for the sake of cheating or the thrill of sex with someone new. But what if you feel a connection to someone—something so deep that you don't know if you can live with the thought that they don't recognize it? Is a conversation considered cheating? What crosses the line? Flirting? Kissing? Sex? What if you still love your husband and your life, but finally accept that your husband is not capable of meeting a particular need? Are you truly required to forego that need forever? Or could it be acceptable, maybe just a bit, to meet it elsewhere if you can find a way to make sure it never hurts him?

I pick up my phone. I have to send this text before I return home if I'm going to do it. I can barely scroll through my contacts because I shake so violently. I'm too chicken to call outright. "You busy tomorrow morning? Need to talk, maybe after I drop the kids at school? Please don't mention it to Ethan." I read it. And reread it. And then I stare at it for about two minutes. And I hit send.

His reply appears almost instantly. "Will do. Is everything all right?"

Is everything all right? That is a loaded question. "It will be. See you tomorrow."

***

I toss and turn all night, trying to figure out how to initiate the conversation. Ethan snuggles up beside me, completely oblivious. His breath warms my shoulder and our toes bump against each other, which is how we always sleep because the weight of even his arm disturbs me. My lack of guilt or conscience surprises me. I just feel nervous, and I revise my speech over and over in my mind, trying to arrange my thoughts.

Chapter 18 ~ November

Ethan kisses me on his way out the door, just like every other morning. I pack up the kids and drop them at school, dressed for the gym as usual. But instead of aiming for the treadmill, my car circles itself back into my driveway. My patience evaporates as I dash back into the house, shower, and slide into tight jeans and a hoodie. I aim to look cute, but not desperate. I text Tad, "Ready whenever."

He responds, "Be over in five minutes."

I perch on the sofa, eyes closed, practicing my speech over and over in my head. I'm really going to do this. I'm going to tell him. And then I'm going to walk away and leave it at that. I won't cheat. I just can't live with the fact that he could leave and never know. His knock on the door jolts me out of my thoughts.

As I open it, my heart picks up pace, and suddenly I'm so nervous that I can't meet his eyes.

"Is everything okay?" he inquires, concern apparent in his face.

"Uh, come on in," I stammer. "I just," my breath hitches, "I need to talk to you for a minute. Come in and sit down."

Tension springs between us and a nervous unease replaces his earlier concern. I hunker into the sofa, legs curled in front of me. He settles in a sleek recliner across the room, looking a bit perplexed. I try to speak but nothing comes out. A long, awkward silence stretches between us and I still can't face him eye to eye.

"Did I do something?" he asks. "Is there something wrong with the electrical or the fan or something?"

"Give me a minute," I plead, and inhale sharply. As I exhale, the words rush out. "This thing, whatever it is, between us—well, it's mutual. Or at least I think it is unless I'm dreaming it from your side. I feel it when you walk into a room. You watch me. And I look for you. When I play with the kids or swim in the pool, I look to see if you're watching. And I look for your car." The vision of his empty parking spot flashes through my mind. "Every time I pull into my driveway, I check to see if you're home. And when you left for St. Louis, I felt like someone punched a hole in my chest and I couldn't breathe. I couldn't breathe because I knew you were with her. I trust you enough to admit this. I'm confiding in you. I'm married, and obviously this gives you the power to destroy that if you choose. And I have no idea why I trust you that much, but I do, because I know you'd never intentionally hurt me." I lace my fingers together, trying to prevent them from visibly shaking. "You need to understand that I love my husband and my family. I'm not saying I don't. But whatever this is, I need to acknowledge it exists. I offer you nothing and don't want to insinuate that anything will happen between us. I don't expect anything. But you will leave, and I need you to know."

Wow. That came out more coherently than I expected except for the tears that filled my eyes when I said the part about him leaving. Damn, I hate to cry. His stunned expression is kind of funny.

"Why are you crying?"

"I have never cheated on Ethan. Never. I actually have never even considered it. This conversation now, this is the first time I've ever violated his trust."

"But we're just talking," he says. "You haven't done anything wrong. You're sitting on the other side of the room from me. How is that cheating?"

"It is. You may not understand, but you haven't been married. To commit to someone requires absolute trust. There can't be any question. You say this conversation isn't cheating, but could I say it in front of Ethan? No, of course not. Simply by speaking, I dishonor him and violate that trust. To break the trust is to break the trust, no matter how you go about it.

"Speaking of which, am I now a interfering with your relationship with the girl you took to St. Louis? I encouraged you to open up to her and now I'm spilling this."

"Ironic," he answers, "but no." A melancholy grimace travels across his face. "She and I agreed just to be friends. Either way, this conversation would have nothing to do with it. I'm flattered. Honestly, flattered isn't enough to describe it. But what made you decide to tell me? And why me?"

"I didn't choose you." I search for words carefully. When I composed my first speech, I failed to envision the remainder of the conversation, which leaves me hunting for an articulate reply. I should have factored that into this plan. Too late now. "It's been there for a while. You can't pretend you never noticed all the innuendo and the silences. And as for why I'm telling you, I don't have a good answer for that one. I replay it over and over it in my head. You left every year for college and it never affected me. You never even crossed my mind. But this summer changed everything, and now you're leaving; you're moving permanently, and I know that you won't be back. That is good. It's supposed to happen. But it also made me realize that things will never be the same again. You won't pop in every time I text for help. Our conversations won't dance around each other. I realized that if you leave now and I don't say something, then you'll never know."

"I feel bad." Tad's eyes drop to the carpet; he flips the corner up and down with his shoe. "I didn't mean to intrude. I wasn't trying to interfere with your marriage. I'm sorry if what I said or did lead you on. The inappropriate comments, well, I didn't—"

"Do you seriously think that no one has approached me before?" My hands shoot out to gesture with a flourish. "I know I'm not perfect, but I stop by the gym most days. I look really young for my age. If you think no one flirted or tried to pick me up in all these years, you'd be mistaken. There have been plenty. The difference is, I've never responded before."

"So why?" he repeats. "Why me?"

"I ask myself the same question. A lot. And I don't know if I actually have an answer. The only thing I can say is that I've known you a long time. You were so young that I never perceived you as a threat. It was just a silly banter. For most people, I keep my walls up pretty high, so compliments or flirting tend to bounce off. But there were never any walls with you. You've been in and out of my life now for so long that when you came back as an adult, it took me by surprise."

"There was a time," he says, "when I thought there was something. But I knew you were married. I knew you had a family. So I knew it couldn't be."

"And it can't." I sigh. "I don't ask you for anything. I don't expect anything. I needed to confess, to know that you understand. And I beg you not to tell anyone. But now when you leave, I can release this emotion and move on."

"I will never tell anyone," he says. "What happens between us stays between us."

I rise and he follows me to the front door. "So now the treadmill awaits to burn off last night's potatoes. Thanks for coming. And for listening. It means more to me than you can know." We stand by my front door, searching each other's eyes. I can tell he doesn't know how to proceed. I don't, either. I want to touch him, but I know I can't. He seems to understand.

He smiles, says, "See you in the driveway," goes out the door, and walks home.

My chest expands. I feel better, lighter. Not exactly how I anticipated, but better. Now I won't sit up at night wondering what would have happened if I told him. I run up the stairs, slip into my running pants, and pull my hair into a high ponytail.

As the garage door opens, I realize my iPod still lies on the kitchen counter. I swivel around to run for the house and there is Tad, not six inches from my face. I jump. "Sheesh, you're quiet. Did you forget something?"

He silently looks straight into my eyes—well, down into my eyes because he's so tall. And staring up, I see what I feel reflected in his. Slowly, he smiles. "Can I come back over tomorrow morning? I'd really like to talk a bit more."

"Sure." My fingers tingle as the flame swells inside me again. "Tomorrow."

Chapter 19 ~ November

"So what else do you want to talk about?" Tad sits in my den again and initiates the conversation. The kids are at school and Ethan is working. He moved to a soft chair that is closer to the sofa, but reclines back in a way that suggests he could be my therapist. Ha.

"Me? You're the one who suggested this again. I covered everything I planned to say yesterday."

"But I don't understand," he interjects. "Did you just realize this yesterday? Have you known for a while? Where did it come from?"

"I don't know," I answer honestly. "I guess I've always been conscious of you, for lack of a better way to phrase it. Most of the time I'm so consumed with myself that I don't notice other people around me, but, for some reason, you were always on the edge of my perception. The first time I acknowledged it developing was back when you offered to take us shooting during the summer. If you remember, we cancelled more than once. At first I agreed, but the more I thought about it, I just couldn't go. I remembered you teaching me to shoot a few summers ago. I didn't want Ethan to go with us. It scared me that he might somehow discern my emotions. But I wouldn't go without him. So I made excuses and cancelled babysitters and then told him they had bailed. I tried everything to avoid the situation all together.

"When Ethan hired you to wire the basement, I didn't want you to do it. I told him that clearly, multiple times. Four contractors bid the job. I tried to convince him to hire anyone but you. But he insisted. He wanted to save money. Didn't you think it was odd that he, who knows nothing about electricity, helped you while I, with my engineering degree, hid upstairs with the kids? I tried to convince myself that if I could stay far enough away from you, this connection would fade away."

"But it didn't," he interrupts with a sigh.

"No. It didn't. When Ethan asked you to look through the basement and measure and we were alone together, I knew I was through. I couldn't deny it to myself anymore. You invited this other girl to homecoming and I was jealous. Jealous of a college ballgame. That is messed up.

"But even then, even knowing what I felt, I blocked it out and encouraged you to pursue someone else. I told you, our conversation yesterday was the closest I have ever come to cheating on Ethan. I mean that. The closest. That discussion was the most I have ever violated his trust. I thought if I pushed it away and held out long enough, you'd leave and that would end it. But I can't stay silent. Every time I see you, every time I pass your car in the driveway or bump into you in a parking lot, it reverberates through me that you are leaving for good. And that connection, the one I haven't felt for so long that I didn't even remember what it felt like, will be gone. So I had to tell you. I had to take the chance, because either way I'll lose you, but one way at least I'll know I was right, it was real. Having you here listening for a few minutes is better than wondering what would have happened and regretting the silence."

As I spill it all out, Tad leans forward in his chair, elbows on his knees, brows furrowed in concentration. "You're right," he admits slowly as his eyes skim the room. "I have thought about it. And, yes, this thing between us is there. Yesterday I had no idea how to react. You took me completely by surprise. When you asked me to come over and not mention it to Ethan, I figured I screwed something up pretty badly, like starting a fire in the basement. I thought you were protecting me by not telling him. So walking into that conversation was the last thing I expected.

"You have to understand, I have no experience with women. My weekend in St. Louis, that was it. My first kiss all the way through. It was the only time I've ever done anything. In college, girls occasionally showed interest, but I knew I'd end up hurting them, so I questioned their intentions and tried to figure out what they were looking for in me. In the end, it was always the same. Once the girls got that close, they lost interest and that was the end of it. So nothing like this has ever happened to me. My life doesn't usually go the way I want it to. Actually, it never does. Reality pretty much just sucks. So instead of avoiding it, I attack it head on. I won't back away from the things that are hard. Instead, I just confront them."

I stop him. "But isn't that a self-fulfilling prophecy? If someone is interested in you and you persuade them out of it, then what do you expect? How can you predict the end before it begins?"

"I just do," he says. "Stella, most people aren't like you. They won't say what they mean or tell me what they want. I won't play those games with girls. If they tell me to go away, I go away. If they tell me they need space, I give them space. I do what they ask me to do and, generally, it makes them angry with me."

Interesting. "So if you can always predict the outcome and you know where things are going, where is this going?" I ask in kind of a smart-ass voice. But truthfully I want to hear his answer. I still haven't figured out the reason he wanted to come back and talk today. He obviously hasn't made a move on me and still sits completely outside my perimeter.

"Well," he says, "it can go one of two ways. Either we stay friends and actually kind of become more than friends, knowing that we both feel the same type of connection, or this ruins it and we don't talk anymore."

"Well put," I reply, "but that isn't an answer. That's like saying there are always three paths: yes, maybe, and no. That doesn't equate to knowing where something is going."

"I'd like to be friends," he says. A chill runs down my arm and every tiny hair stands on end at his words.

"Friends," I say. "Like real friends? Like I don't have to pull a fan out of my ceiling to come up with an excuse to persuade you to come over and hang out with me friends? You mean we'll talk other than in the driveway and stuff?"

"Yes," he says. "Friends. And you didn't really pull that bathroom fan out just to get me to come over, did you?" He cracks a smile.

"Well, not entirely. It did actually need to be done. Having you over was just an added benefit." I grin in return.

Over the next few days, Tad manages to insert himself into my daily life. I never expected him to, but I can't say that I mind. He texts almost every day, shows up at my house at random times, and brushes my arm or shoulder as we pass in public. We spend almost every morning together talking. Honestly, I don't even know what we talk about. I just know that when I'm with him, nothing else exists. And I don't notice how much of my life I'm starting to put off to make time for him.

Chapter 20 ~ November

Ethan comes down the stairs looking like a cross between a navy seal and a black crayon. "Like it?" he asks, smiling under what must be the strangest looking ensemble I've ever seen assembled for the astronomical price of three hundred dollars.

"What the hell are you wearing?" He looks ridiculous. He models black running tights, black shorts, a black compression turtleneck, black gloves, and some type of black hood that covers everything except his eyes.

Zach enters the room, squeals, and shrieks, "Daddy's a robber!" over and over. Maya charges up the stairs to see what is going on and collapses in a laughing fit onto the floor. He looks more like a giant condom than a robber.

"This is it," Ethan says. "I'm ready to go. Mark is picking me up. I wanted you to see this before we take off." Ethan anticipates all of his athletic events, but these crazy endurance races are a whole new extreme, even for him. He runs half a marathon, in extremely cold weather, while suffering through various obstacles like ice water baths and electrified fences. It makes no sense to me whatsoever why we pay good money for him to torture himself, but if this is the worst of his mid-life crisis, I should probably be thankful and let him enjoy it. They'll trek off to West Virginia somewhere, spend the night, and return tomorrow.

Usually I miss Ethan when he's gone. I don't like to sleep alone and it scares me to be in the house by myself at night. But tonight I'm fine with it. Maya, Zach, and I returned an hour ago from visiting the Children's Science Center. We left to give Ethan time to pack all of his stuff. Now I'm exhausted. Two kids in a science center are enough to push me in the direction of the nearest bar.

We started in the space section, which was low-key and enjoyable. Then we giggled our way through ice cream, overhead unicycle rides, and volunteering for demonstrations. For the finale, Zach sprayed himself in the face and soaked most of his clothes in the undersea world. Up until that point, things had gone relatively smoothly, but my little drama king killed it. It took me almost thirty minutes to convince him that he could walk to the car in dripping pants without fear of imminent death. He sniffled and snorted the entire drive home, while Maya sat in her corner sulking that we had to leave before our scheduled building time in the gears and widgets section.

I turn on a movie to keep Maya and Zach quiet. They don't even move when Ethan kisses them good-bye. As he approaches the front door he stops, turns to me, drops his bag, and swoops me up in a giant hug.

"Don't get too lonely tonight," he says. "I'll call you when we check in so you know we made it. And I'll see you tomorrow afternoon."

We open the door and walk toward Mark's car in the driveway. "Remember," I say, speaking up so both men can hear me, "no injuries. We can't afford for you to be disabled. Come home safe or die. Those are your options."

"Don't worry. I'll endure less torture than you'll suffer being here." Ethan laughs, pecks me again on the lips, and climbs into the car.

Thankfully, Maya and Zach are good and tired after our excursion. We heat up a freezer pizza and watch a Disney classic until it's time for bed. They don't even complain about the early bedtime on the weekend, so I know they'll pass out. I plan to stay awake for a while, but after saying prayers in their dark rooms, I give it up. I grab my cell phone and stick it by the bed so that it will wake me up when Ethan checks in. It's only eight o'clock.

"What the hell is that buzzing?" I wipe my eyes and try to figure out where I am. Ten seconds ago I was eight years old and walking a tightrope in a circus while my parents told me that they were leaving me there and I could never come home again. Oh, there's my clock. It's only ten thirty now. And my cell phone is about to vibrate off the table.

I flip it open and a new text from Tad flashes. I'd mentioned to him earlier in the week that Ethan would be gone this evening, but it was just flirting, not an invitation. He knew that I planned to be out most of the day. "Home yet?" he asks.

"Yep," I text back. I'm really too tired to have a conversation. I fall back asleep. Literally. With the phone in my hand.

"What are you doing?" comes the reply. The buzz of the phone jolts me awake again.

"Sleeping."

My eyes close again and I'm already nodding off when he texts back. "What are you wearing?"

Really? Could this be any cheesier? What are we, sixteen? Wait, I guess that wasn't so long ago for him. The truth is, I'm wearing my Hanna Andersson flowered long johns with my hair pulled up in a bun and a retainer on my teeth, but there is no way I'm telling *him* that. "Nothing," I respond. Because I know that's the answer he wants. And it's much more fun this way.

"Seriously?" he texts back. "You sleep with nothing on?"

"Sometimes. I am married. You realize that I do actually have sex with my husband, right? So, yes, I sleep naked at least half the time." That was a long text for me. I hate texting more than a few words. "If you want a conversation," I continue before hitting the send button, "call me. I'm tired."

I shut the phone and immediately it rings. "So you were asleep, naked in bed, huh?"

"Yep. Every guy's fantasy. Where are you?"

"In my car, driving home," he says. "I've been out buying everything I need to take with me when I move so that hopefully my parents will pay for it."

"Good plan." I'm still lying on my pillow and feeling pretty comfortable.

There is silence for a minute, and then he quietly adds, "Well, I guess it is my fantasy."

"Huh?" He lost me.

"You," he says. "Naked. If I'm lucky, maybe in the shower."

I consider this. "The shower? You do realize that you're like seven feet tall. I'm only a little over five and a half. How exactly do you think that's going to work?"

"I don't know. I've never tried it. But I'd like to."

Time to steer the conversation in another direction. A little banter and flirting are good, but I don't want to tease him into thinking something is going to happen. We both already agreed that it won't.

"I just pulled into the driveway," he continues. "You wouldn't believe how warm it is out here. It's never like this in November. You should come out."

"Come out? I have two kids asleep in their rooms. Where do you think I'm going to go?"

"How about out in the yard to talk?" He issues the invitation hesitantly. "That way we won't wake them up."

I mull it over. I don't want to invite Tad into my house in the middle of the night while Ethan's out of town. I think inside, in the dark, we might cross lines and confuse things pretty quickly. But I'm awake now thanks to him. I peer out the window; the full moon illuminates the entire yard, so there's plenty of light.

"How warm?" I ask. "Light jacket or T-shirt?"

"T-shirt," he says. I frantically sift through my drawers, searching for bras and panties that match. Am I seriously matching my underwear to sit in the yard and talk? But something inside me does it anyway. I pull out the retainer, run a brush through my hair, and slide into a sweatshirt and jeans.

"Okay. I'm walking out my front door." And I am. I go out the front door and around the side of the house. Tad's Corolla sits in the driveway but I don't see him anywhere. "Where the hell are you?"

"Okay, seriously," he says sarcastically.

"No, asshole," I laugh. "I'm sitting in my backyard by myself. You think I'm joking? You're the one who invited me, right?"

"No way." Over the phone, I hear him shuffling and then the back door of his house creaks open. "Are you really out here?" Now I hear him through the phone and in stereo.

"Walk this way," I direct him. "Toward my house, a little more, up the hill—"

He sees me and we simultaneously disconnect the call. He approaches me, but doesn't sit. Instead, he mills around in aimless circles.

"I can't believe you actually came out here," he says. "I thought you were joking."

"At first I was, but then I figured what the hell, now I'm awake and I don't have anything else to do."

My words trail off into silence. He is a shadow with the moon behind him. I can feel him looking at me, not knowing what to do or say next. I have no idea, either.

"You can sit down," I offer, patting the ground beside me. "I promise I won't bite." His uncertain expression amplifies the silence as he meets my eyes and sits. The seconds expand. My stomach flip flops and I start to shake.

"Are you cold?" he asks. "You look like you're vibrating."

"Not cold," I answer, "just nervous."

And with that, he bends his head down toward me and, as our noses brush, murmurs, "I'm not very good at this. I don't have much practice."

"Shut up," I respond, and a moment later his lips touch mine. I almost laugh because it is so chaste. No tongue, no passion, just a peck kiss on the lips that he seems to want to hold there. He really doesn't have any idea what he is doing. But inside me, the adrenaline pumps furiously. I quiver like a tuning fork and realize that I haven't had a first kiss in over fourteen years. I'm as much a virgin to this as he is. But the difference is that I know how to channel that smoldering. "Come here," I murmur right next to his lips, and the next moment I slide my hand up to grasp his neck, push his mouth open, and ram in my tongue.

He sharply draws his breath, and his pressure increases to match mine almost immediately. His arms wrap around me as he lays me back in the grass. The more intense he becomes, the more my body responds. He may not have experience, but he's quick on the uptake. My abdominal muscles contract as I arch my back and push myself against him. My body shakes. The combination of fear, longing, and exhilaration is indescribable. I remember this feeling. It is the me from long ago. The me who existed before the mundane days of marriage pushed me into routine sex. The me who existed before the children hemmed me in under the name "Mom". The me who existed before responsibility weighed me down into the earth.

Anyone could walk up at any time. Hell, his brother could pull into the driveway and illuminate us in a giant spotlight. But I don't care. I can't think past wanting him to kiss me again.

He pulls back. "You're shaking really hard. Are you okay?"

"More than okay," I say, and he rolls over and pulls me into his arms. We alternate talking, making out, and gazing at the stars.

At one point, he asks, "So do you think you'll ever leave him?"

"I don't know. Yes, I think. But the problem isn't leaving him; it's dismantling our life. I have so many responsibilities. It doesn't just affect me and him. It takes everything we've built with it—our finances, our stability, the consistency for the kids...."

"I wish you were younger. I wish we could actually give this a chance."

"Same here. If you were forty, I'd walk out the door and wouldn't look back. But you're not. And married or single, my responsibilities and commitments don't go away. At twenty-three, you aren't ready to raise someone else's kids. You have things you need to do with your life. So do I."

"But what will happen if you leave him?" he pushes further.

"You need to understand, Tad. My relationship with Ethan is completely separate from what we have. He's my family, just like your parents are yours. We've been together so long that I don't remember my life without him. I love him, even if I'm not in love with him. You need to accept that if I stay with him, it doesn't negate anything I feel for you. And that if I leave him, it isn't for you. It will be for me. Ethan and I had problems before you and I ever knew each other. Either way, this is completely separate."

Other than kissing me, he doesn't make any inappropriate moves or press me physically any further. He never asks to come in the house.

"I need to go back inside," I say after what seems like hours. "I don't have a monitor out here and even though the kids almost always sleep through the night, I'd feel awful if one of them had a nightmare and they walked into my room to find me gone."

We stand and I brush the grass clippings from my pants. "So I'll see you early next week? Because we're leaving mid-week to visit my parents for Thanksgiving."

"Sounds like a plan," he agrees. He starts toward his back door but I grab his hand just before he is out of range. When he turns, he pushes me back into the fence and presses his mouth into mine. I can feel that his body wants mine as much as mine wants his. I entangle my tongue in his, slipping over and around his teeth, and we both pull away while we can.

"Good night Tad," I whisper. And I walk back into my house without looking back.

The minute I creep through the door, I hear crying in Zach's room. I run up the steps, but he's sleeping, having a nightmare. I sit beside his bed and smooth his hair back, kissing his forehead and singing to him. But my mind is still sitting in my backyard.

When Zach quiets down, I return to my room. In the glare of the bathroom light, I see the grass in my hair and the dirt on my sweatshirt. Guess that means I'll need to throw in some laundry tomorrow morning. I hop into the shower, letting it run over me as hot as I can stand it, and run my hands along my body, imagining they are his.

It isn't until I emerge from the shower and settle back into bed, this time actually naked, that I notice my phone, which dropped by my pillow when I undressed, flashing 2:36 a.m. There is a voice mail from Ethan. "Made it here safely, but went out for dinner and didn't check into the hotel until late. Sure you're already asleep by now since I know you were wiped. Thanks for keeping the kids out of my way today. Love you. See you tomorrow."

Chapter 21 ~ November

The next few days blur together. School winds down for the holiday, but somehow Tad and I steal hours between the kids' Pilgrim and Indian classroom parties. Kissing and snuggling replace our conversations, but Tad doesn't push for anything more. We both understand our relationship can't go anywhere. His two weeks left at home speed by.

Over Thanksgiving, Ethan and I drag the kids to my parents' house in Kentucky. I can't say I enjoy any of the trip. Most of the time, I'm thinking of Tad. I try to push him from my mind, focus on the present, and distract myself with the kids. It doesn't help that Ethan and I never have sex in my parents' house. It makes me uncomfortable. But right now, I need sex with him almost constantly. I tell myself that as long as Ethan and I are intimate, as long as he is the one I come home to at the end of the day, the rest of this can be forgiven; although I don't intend to tell him what is happening and test out that theory.

We haven't been home an hour when Tad stops by to drop off our mail. "Tomorrow morning, then?" he asks. Upstairs, Ethan stows away the kids' pillows, books, and stuffed animals.

"Okay." I smile. We managed to sneak in a few text messages here and there while I was gone, but now that I'm back in the same room with him, the familiar warmth takes hold.

The next morning, following my routine of hustling Ethan and the kids out the door, Tad arrives. "This time we actually need to talk," he blurts as he surfaces for air fifteen minutes later.

"Yes," I answer seductively. He sits on the sofa and I perch on his lap, facing him with my legs spread around his waist, more than a little distracted.

"How far are we letting this go?" he questions. "At first I thought it was just going to be friendship. Then we crossed that line. Then we kissed and I thought it would stop there. But we're close to crossing that line. How far are you willing to let this go?"

I sigh and collect my thoughts as I slide back a little to look at him. "I'm not sure," I finally confess. "I didn't plan for any of this. In the beginning, truly all I wanted was to tell you. I wanted to take one final chance in my life because at this point I take so few of them. But the more time we spend together, the more I want. I guess if I'm completely honest, I expected you'd kiss me when I went outside that Saturday while Ethan was gone. And by the time we got to that point, I'd made my peace with it. I thought kissing you would end it. I've kissed plenty of people with no chemistry whatsoever. And, since it's been so long since I've kissed anyone but Ethan, I assumed it would kind of suck, and that would be the end of it. Maybe that isn't what you want to hear, but that's really what I thought. Then it didn't. We came together in a way that I never anticipated. So now I don't know what I want. Obviously, at least part of me wants to go further. But even if we did, I couldn't do it here in my house. That would be too much. We'd have to go somewhere else. I mean, how long until you actually leave?"

"Stella," he sighs and closes his eyes. I still sit on top of him, our foreheads pressed together and noses touching. "I leave on Monday."

Monday. This is happening. He is leaving. And it isn't for a few days away or a college semester. Tad is moving to the other side of the country. There will never be another summer when he drops in to help with projects or another afternoon to bump into him in the driveway. There will be no more long conversations where he completely distracts me as I take out the trash.

Part of me is crushed. But a voice inside, a tiny one, tells me this is for the best. Yes, these crazy, powerful feelings for Tad overwhelm me, but they haven't wrecked my marriage. Yet. In the middle of my den, the den in the house that Ethan and I bought together, I cling to this other man and wonder how I'm going to let him go. Every piece of furniture in the room is something Ethan and I selected and purchased together. He doesn't deserve this.

My entire line of thinking dissipates when Tad opens his eyes and peers into mine. "So we only have a couple more days," he continues.

"Actually, not all of them," I respond, resting my chin on his shoulder and turning what started as a seductive pose into a half hug, half slump. "I volunteered to help at the school tomorrow morning with a reading celebration."

"My dad scheduled vacation on Wednesday to help me pack and we load the moving van on Thursday, so both of those days are hectic for me," he says. I watch the switch flip in his eyes as we both realize what this means. He transforms from being close with me one moment to gone the next. He moves into a mode where he is all business, where nothing that is said can hurt him.

"So that leaves what? Friday?" I ask.

"Friday," he confirms. "We leave at six on Monday morning."

I squirm off his lap and pull my legs up to my chest, maybe trying to block the giant hole forming there. "So what you're saying is if we decide to sleep together, it has to be Friday? How is that supposed to work? We have sex once, you leave, and I never see or hear from you again?" I'm scared. He puts me in an impossible position. As far back as I can remember, I've never wanted anything like I want him.

"No," Tad analyzes our options. "It means that we're friends. And if we both want this, if we both agree to never tell anyone and black out a few hours of our lives, then we can have that."

"I'm not like that, Tad." The tears push through, and I struggle to hold them back. "I don't fling. I have never cheated on my husband. I can't separate what I feel from being close to you. The thought that I'd betray Ethan just to 'black out' a few hours isn't enough for me. When I have sex, it's body and soul. There is no other way for me. And if that isn't what it is, if it isn't two people who have such a strong connection that they need the physical to express the emotional, then it isn't anything."

He bears down on top of me, pushing me back into the sofa and driving his mouth onto mine. I immediately arch into him. His legs force mine apart as he shifts his weight onto me. We are both fully clothed, but I feel completely exposed. His hands roam, first around my shoulders and back, then tentatively, in direct opposition to the force he is exerting with his mouth and the rest of his body, he timidly runs his hand along the side of my breast. My patience evaporates. I need him to touch me. I grab both his hands, place each one directly around a breast, and squeeze. "It's okay," I murmur, and he doesn't ask twice. In the back of my mind, I wonder if this is it. I can't deny that I want him. But I can't make that call. I can't say yes. He has not attempted to touch me below the waist or remove my pants. He waits for me, giving me space to signal that I'm ready. I can't.

The heat quietly dissipates and, between kisses, Tad pulls back to adjust himself.

"I'm not sure I can do this." I huddle into my corner of the sofa. "Don't misunderstand me. I want to. I really want to. But I haven't been with anyone but Ethan in more than," I stop and calculate, "over fourteen years." Holy shit. I just said that out loud. I met Ethan when Tad was nine years old. That kind of brings things into perspective. "What if we start and I can't go through with it? What if the minute my clothes come off, I panic?"

"I've considered that," Tad responds. "That's why we're taking this so slow. I'm moving at your pace and I won't press any further than you want. I won't push you into it."

"I can't give you an answer. You understand that, right?" I ask. "The situation, the mood, the connection between us determines it all. But you have to understand that if I say yes, and if it does happen, it involves a connection, not a couple of blacked-out hours."

"I know that." He sighs wistfully. "I was wrong to say otherwise. I just didn't know how to phrase it. And now, I need to go. I scheduled to meet someone for lunch. Since it's my last week, it seems everyone wants to say good-bye."

"Until Friday then," I say. I realize this is it. Tad will walk out my door today, I will see him on Friday, and he will disappear. He pulls me into one more hug, which develops into a kiss, and he backs me into the wall. We stop simultaneously.

"Friday," he says. He pecks me on the mouth and leaves.

Chapter 22 ~ November

Over the next few days, exercise comforts my mind as I blast the music on my iPod, pushing myself harder and harder while processing thoughts of Tad. I schedule lunches with friends for both days that Tad is occupied because I cannot remain in the house and watch him load the moving van. My mind leaps from one decision to the other almost every hour. I know that I am capable of going through with it now, but I haven't decided if I want to.

By Thursday morning, I'm a wreck. Sleep eludes me, as does a decision. After exercising, I meet Alyssa for burgers and milkshakes. While we lunch, she drones on and on, describing her job search, her problems with her ex-husband, and her worries about her daughter. I'm glad she has plenty to say because my mind refuses to follow the conversation. It is hard to sit across from her, wanting her advice so badly, but not able to ask for it. But this is too big to trust anyone with, even her. Finally, my opening arrives, so I initiate the conversation casually.

"Did you ever feel tempted to cheat on Josh? Did you ever feel like someone else was pushing too far into your life?" Josh is her second husband. Her first marriage ended almost before it began, immediately following high school.

"Of course, sweetie," she says. "Don't you remember my online card games back when Ashley started school? I was bored to death. I played games to pass the time. A guy I met there, Will, always logged in at the same time as me. At first it was friendly chit-chat, but we quickly progressed to intimate confessions in private chat rooms. I knew it was wrong, but I assumed this nameless, faceless guy on the computer couldn't hurt anything. So I encouraged it. He made me feel funny, pretty, smart, and all those other things that Josh used to make me feel. Every day, I waited for the time when I could go online and chat with Will, until he demanded naked pictures of me. I refused to send them and he threatened to call Josh and turn over a record of all of our chats and emails. I realized what I'd done, how much I'd risked for some guy that I knew really nothing about."

"So did you just stop?"

"Yes," she says, but I can tell I'm not hearing the whole truth. "It wasn't easy. I prayed about it every day and I panicked every time the phone rang. Finally, I felt trapped. I confessed the whole thing to Josh. I explained to him how I missed him and how it made me feel when I was stuck at home alone. I apologized and begged him not to leave me. And he didn't. He forgave me and our marriage has been better since. He understands my needs a little more and tries to fill them now." She plucks another roll from the basket. "Why?"

I know I can't tell her the truth, but some modification of the truth should work Almost all of our good friends have heard about Tad at one time or another, either when Ethan refers to him as my boyfriend as the punch line of some joke over dinner or in passing comments concerning one of the many projects that he has done around our house.

"Remember the neighbors' kid from next door, Tad?" I ask. She nods, so I continue. "Well, he kind of hit on me." It feels wrong rolling out of my mouth, because it was the other way around. "And it's okay. I didn't do anything. But I wanted to and that scared me. It made me question what's lacking in my life and in my marriage that would allow me to consider it."

Empathy pours through her smile. "You and Ethan will be fine. You guys are strong. Yes, the enemy sends people into our lives to tempt us, people who look like exactly what we need. But God bound you to the man you are supposed to be with. So you need to trust that. Trust that he knew what he was doing when he put the two of you together."

Oh, crap. Alyssa's religious doctrines insert themselves between us immediately. When we met, we shared similar beliefs. Over the past year or so, her religion first enveloped and then defined her. I don't know what inside her caused such desperation, but we grow apart as she immerses deeper and deeper into her presumptive theology.

She drones on and on about how the enemy attacks me and I tune her out. This reminds me why we don't have lunch as frequently as we used to.

Then she jerks me back into reality. "The enemy is attacking you the only way he can. You and Ethan guard your marriage. You are both on the lookout. You don't allow people to interfere in your lives. So he attacks with what he knows is your greatest weakness. You have a weakness for Tad. You always have. But a line remained between you that, because of age and circumstance, you never would have considered crossing. But now your life has changed, and the enemy sees it. He sees opportunities to exploit your weakness and prey on all of your fears—the fears of feeling alone, growing older, and losing yourself."

She is right. Completely, absolutely right. Not about the enemy crap, because a devil certainly has more important things to do than stalk me, but correct in inferring that this is my greatest weakness. That perhaps I need my eyes opened to see it clearly. I *am* aging. I assume that men find me attractive because they always have. But now a different demographic looks in my direction. It isn't the twenty-year-olds scoping me out at the bar anymore. Hell, I could be their mother. I somehow morphed into a minivan-driving mom with a schedule consisting of laundry, cooking, and elementary school homework. I contracted into a sphere of support to allow Ethan, Maya, and Zach to expand. But there has to be something left in me to support everyone else, and right now it isn't there.

Tad is my weakness. He flatters me. He listens to me. He rides in on his white horse to rescue me every time I need help. He makes me feel important. He is in the position to be all the things that Ethan can't be for me.

We finish our lunch with small talk. Opening up relieved my tension a bit, even if it was mostly a lie. I think I found the response I needed out of it, though.

Thursday night I toss and turn for hours, totally unable to sleep. While Ethan snores beside me, I start to pray silently. "God, you know I stink at praying and don't know the right words to say. But you also know what is in my heart. I have no idea what is happening here. I am lying next to the man I love. But I am lonely. I have given up everything for him and for Maya and Zach. I gave up my career. Sacrificed my body. There is nothing left either inside me or around me that is just mine. And with Tad, I find myself. It is selfish, something I'm not forced to share with anyone else, something that is all mine, even if it is just a feeling. So now I don't even know what to pray for. Do I pray for the strength to say no tomorrow? The truth is, I don't want to say no. Do I pray that you allow me this once to keep something for myself? I don't know. So all I can ask is that you take my burden, help me sleep, and let me find my way tomorrow. Because no matter what decision I make, I can't do it on my own."

***

Friday morning I'm geared up. As I dress, I ensure my underwear matches under my exercise pants and hoodie. I drop utensils as I prepare the kids' breakfasts and I snap at them when they ask for gloves because the weather is cooling off. I hide in the bathroom to grunt a good-bye as Ethan leaves for work instead of kissing him.

Finally, everyone is gone and I'm alone. I'm shaking. I switch my phone on and off. When I woke up this morning, I knew my answer. Yes. I want to be close to Tad, even if it must be contained in this small moment. I begin the text to invite him over; the front door is already unlocked. But I shake too violently and my fingers won't hit the right letters. I delete and try again. I can't do it. Finally, I suck in a deep breath and call him. He picks up on the first ring.

"You home?"

"Yes," I answer. "But we need to talk first." The tears spill over, but I push through my words as fast as I can. "Tad, I have to ask you not to come over this morning. The problem is, well, the answer is yes. Yes, Tad. If you walk through that door, I'm going to start something I can't stop. And I won't want to stop it. But I can't do it. As much as I want this, as much as I want you, I can't. And it's not about Ethan. This is about us. You'll leave on Monday and I may never hear from you or see you again. You'll start an entirely new life, one that I'm not a part of. But you have to understand that I won't. On Monday I'll still be sitting here. And that's the way it's supposed to happen. I'm not angry or upset; I didn't expect it to end differently. I'll go back to my days and life as if this never happened, and that's hard enough for me. I won't make it harder on myself when I already know that I'll have to let you go."

Tad's silence disturbs me. I can't even hear him breathing. "Can I at least come over and talk then?" he finally asks.

"No. I can't talk, at least not now. I need time. So maybe I'll call you later, or find you over the weekend, but right now, no."

"Okay," he says dully.

"Bye, Tad." I hang up the phone as I choke back a sob. But I can't hold it back for long. Before I know it, I'm balled on the floor, sobbing with a hurt that I haven't felt in so long that I didn't remember what it felt like. The hole inside me expands through my chest and under my ribs as I realize how far I've allowed myself to slip. I try to calm myself, but I cry, a violent, gut-wrenching choke, for over an hour.

Then I hear it. A knock on the door. I swallow my breath, walk to the front of the house, and open it.

Tad isn't standing on my front porch like normal. He paces in the driveway, hands in his pockets, eyes downcast, looking rumpled and worried. He barely makes eye contact. "I wanted to make sure you're okay," he says. I can't decide if he really means it or if he thinks I might still invite him inside. Right now I'm too broken to think.

"I'm not," I say, "but I will be. I'll see you later, okay?" I shut the door, walk upstairs, and fall onto my bed.

A few hours later, I wake up and eat lunch. As my thoughts clear, I realize that I just wasted my last private hours with Tad. I might bump into him over the weekend, but Ethan will be around. I check the clock. Half an hour remains before I have to retrieve the kids from school. Should I try to talk to him? I guess I could at least apologize if nothing else.

I shoot him a text. "You busy?"

His response is immediate. "Nope."

"Can you stop by?"

There is no reply, but a knock at my door announces his arrival.

"Sorry about earlier," I apologize as he comes in. "I just needed some time. The pressure was too much."

"I know," he comforts me. "I knew it Monday when we talked and realized that today would be our last day together. I saw what it did to you. And you shouldn't make this decision under a time constraint. I'm happy that you even thought to answer yes, that you considered me. Honestly, I never truly believed I had a chance, so just the fact that you went that far means a great deal to me."

"So I guess this is it then," I say.

"Maybe. I'm sure I'll swing by a few times this weekend. I have some things I want to drop off for Ethan and I promised I'd help him with a last minute project. We planned to leave at six on Monday, but may push it off until a little later. I'd prefer not to wake up that early just to drive. I told my parents that I scheduled breakfast with a friend and that we'd leave afterward. They weren't too thrilled, so I don't know if I can delay them or not. But if I can, I might be able to stop by on Monday morning."

"Yes, I would like to spend another morning with you if we can drop the expectations. I'm not promising anything. But if you need to leave, that's okay. too. I guess it means I have to kiss you good-bye now."

It is beautiful and passionate and sad. But I am intact. I am intact because I do not regret anything that happened. Tad respected my decisions. For the first time today, I feel like I am going to be all right. I am going to make it through this in one piece.

Chapter 23 ~ December

The weekend passes too quickly. Tad spends as much time at my house as he does at his own. He stops over every few hours, using our computer or offering a helping hand as his excuse to visit. I suspect that being here helps him separate from his family, but I know that part of him wants to be close to me. And although I should object, I crave his attention, even if it means discussing computer problems.

Ethan brings him up in conversation repeatedly, which unnerves me. I think Tad's imminent departure has almost as much effect on Ethan as it does me. Maybe it makes both of us feel older. Or maybe it just forces us to acknowledge that we're trapped. The life we built together has become our cage—a gilded cage, but a cage nonetheless. Either way, Ethan's comments confound me. He asks if I'm sad because my boyfriend is leaving. He devises last-minute projects and asks me to text him almost hourly.

Sunday, as Tad walks out the door after popping in to reset our iPod for the eighty-fourth time, he turns to me. "We're leaving later tomorrow. I'll see you in the morning?"

"Yep," is all I can say. But I'm happy. This is the same guy I turned down on Friday. The one whose face I shut the door in. He is still making the effort, carving out time to see me even when I wasted the time I should have appreciated. I don't plan to have sex with him and I'm certain he knows it. But I still can't wait until tomorrow morning.

***

Monday I fall back into my usual routine. I kiss Ethan good-bye, drive the kids to school, pull into the garage, and text Tad. He jumps as soon as I call. Today, there is no small talk as he walks through the door. He kisses me right in front of the window, where anyone, including his parents, could easily see us. I grab his hand and lead him away. We don't make it down the stairs before he turns and rams his mouth against mine again. This time, there is no pulling away. On the step, I closely approach his height. His hands run up and down my back, then drop, feeling along the rim of my black lace underwear and making me twitch in anticipation. As he thrusts his tongue into my mouth, his hands slide down the back of my pants and firmly grasp my ass. He pulls, lifting me until our heights are equivalent. I wrap my legs around his waist as he pushes his mouth more and more feverishly against mine. Without stopping, he slowly turns and makes his way to the sofa, holding me the entire time. "Hold on tight," he whispers as we topple over. There are no other words because there is no time, no breath. He grinds into me through our clothing. My nipples tighten under my shirt and I arch, wanting him so badly that I already anticipate what he will feel like inside me. His hands slide up and down my chest under my shirt, exploring and teasing, but his mouth is relentless and leaves me gasping for breath.

He pauses for a moment, smiles slightly, and unbuttons his shirt. "It's a little hot, don't you think?" he asks. His button-down lands on the coffee table. "Oh, and the phone is uncomfortable." He unfastens his belt and unloads his pockets. Phone. Watch. Knife. Handcuff keys. Wait. What the hell?

"You carry handcuff keys? Is this on an everyday basis or just because you thought you might need them with me?"

"I carry them every day," he answers with a seriousness I honestly can't believe. "You know my dad's a prison guard. You never know when you might need them."

Wow. That leads to a whole level of paranoia that I have no interest in considering—or to a lot of expectation for the next few hours. Either way, it rattles me. The heat dissipates and I look from him to the clock.

"So what time do you have to leave?"

"I told Dad I'd be home by ten," he says. "I'm sure he's pacing, waiting for me to walk in the door." We've been together for over an hour. "So, to the basement?" He stands and grasps my hand to lead me down the stairs. I don't budge.

"Well?" His eyebrows raise as he attempts to persuade me. He knows I fantasize about having sex with him in my basement. We disclosed fantasies in some late night phone conversation long ago. The rest of the house is too connected to my family and Ethan. But I almost never spend time in the basement, which makes it easier to picture myself there with him.

"Tad, no," I answer. "Yes, I want to be with you. Yes, I want to have sex with you more than you can possibly imagine. But, no, we are not going to my basement to do it. First, I told you it couldn't be in my house and it still can't be. This is my home with Ethan. I allowed you to go this far, but I cannot be intimate with you here. And, second, we only have an hour. If I recall, your St. Louis date took almost two hours?" His embarrassed expression answers for him, so I continue. "I can guarantee that it won't take two hours because I actually know what I'm doing," I take a deep breath before I proceed, "but I'm not willing to rush any more than I was willing to rush into it Friday. The right thing occurs at the right time. If it's right, it'll happen, but not today and not now."

He releases my hands to push me back down on the sofa, pressing himself against me as his tongue communicates his response. I'll interpret that as a positive sign that he isn't offended. As we meld together and kiss, I can't say that I don't rethink my decision several times. But it is made, and I am committed to it.

Finally, he pulls away. "It's almost time for me to go," he says. He reloads his pockets and then shakes out his rumpled shirt before pulling it back on. I lay on the sofa without adjusting my position and watch. I long to memorize his face, his smell, his feel… I snap a mental picture to carry with me when I regret saying no. Because I foresee a time when I will.

When he meets my eyes, only once, I glimpse tears. They may be because of his feelings for me, or might just accompany his realization that he's leaving his life here for good. In an instant he blinks them away. It was so fast that if I hadn't watched so closely, I would have missed them all together.

"You know I'm kind of falling in love with you, right?" I speak the words quietly. "And you're leaving. And that's what you're supposed to do. So don't worry. You may not know exactly where you're headed, but you'll own the place in ten years."

He smiles tenderly and leans in for one last kiss. "Good-bye Stella," he says. "I'll keep in touch."

"I'm counting on it. Good-bye Tad."

As soon as he crosses the yard, I jump into my van and fly out of the drive. I can't sit in my house and watch him leave. Emotion overwhelms me. I go where I always go when I need to process: to the gym. Up until the past few weeks, I spent almost every morning after I dropped Maya and Zach at school in the gym. But somehow, with Tad, I let my routine slide. Now it's time to run. If I can't run away, I will run the pain and frustration out of my system until I accept my circumstances. Alone.

By the time I return, Tad's Corolla has vanished from the driveway. I feel like I've been punched in the chest. I have a sinking suspicion that I'm going to experience this sensation a lot. For the remainder of the afternoon, I immerse myself in activity. I have to fill this gaping hole with something, so I attempt to occupy my mind with busy work.

Late in the afternoon, while I help Maya with her science homework, he texts me. "Made it halfway to the hotel. Dad is driving me crazy in the car. I miss you already."

"I miss you, too," I reply. And I do, but instead of with desperate longing, it's more of a pleasant warmth, a reminder of our time together. I return to Maya's homework.

Chapter 24 ~ December

I wonder what Tad is doing. Last Friday, only a week ago, he knocked on my door and I turned him away. Over the past week, my life has returned to something that resembles normal. Ethan and I are actually getting along much better than we did before everything with Tad started. I can't figure out what generated the shift. Perhaps the fact that I've released Ethan from all expectations? I can't tell.

Earlier today while Ethan worked, I set up a separate email address for private communication with Tad. Once he starts his job, our opportunities to talk during the day will rapidly diminish, and I hope this will provide a way for us to stay in touch.

He texted a few times, but has been busy selecting an apartment and settling in. His parents stayed to assist with his transition and intrude on his free time. Most of our messages revolve around what might have happened if we had sex. Or flirt with the possibility of it still happening.

In the strobe light, base thumping, I shoot him a text. "Some PTA idiot volunteered me to chaperone a junior high dance. Watching the kids orbit each other is hysterical. What are you up to?"

My phone dings almost instantaneously. "Just got off work. Swinging by home to change and then meeting friends for dinner."

"Sounds fun. People from work?"

"Yep. I'm supposed to be there in fifteen minutes."

A pubescent boy, complete with acne and a fedora, approaches me. "Watch this," he announces before throwing himself into a krump, impressively done, at that. Since he isn't holding—or maybe isn't interested in—the attention of girls his age, he's moved on to the nearest adult for encouragement.

"Nice," I nod my head and return to my phone. "Sorry for the delay. Some kid wanted me to watch him dance. They do occasionally require supervision."

"Picking up younger men?" Tad jokes.

"Exactly. That's all I do in my spare time. But this crowd would land me in jail," I type, followed by a smiley emoticon. "Aren't you supposed to be at dinner?"

"I'm late."

"I'll let you go then." He needs to make new friends, not hang on the phone with me. I miss him, but these snippets of his life comfort me. "I don't want to intrude," I continue. "Just thought I'd say hi."

"You could never bother me," he responds. I catch my breath and feel him surrounding me. My phone dings again. "Want to talk?" The words, although there are only three of them, slam into me, calling up memories of gazing into his eyes as he proposed that same question in my garage. They remind me that someone in this universe grasps me, even from a distance.

"I can't right now. I have to provide a barrier for all the raging hormones in the room."

"Because that's your specialty?"

"Obviously. I blocked yours didn't I?"

"Maybe we can talk this weekend?"

Between the kids and Ethan, there isn't much free time. "Ethan is running a race on Sunday morning. I can call you then, but it will be the crack of dawn your time."

"Anytime. I'll be waiting."

***

Sunday morning, I lie in bed silently. The front door smacks shut. The garage door mechanism hums. Ethan's SUV engine fires and moments later he is gone. The clock glows 7:13 a.m. here, three hours earlier Tad's time. It seems ridiculous not to wait until later to call, but I don't want to.

"You up?" Naked, wrapped in my sheet, I text instead of dialing, grinning at the innuendo. I don't actually expect him to be awake or answer.

"I am now," he replies only seconds later. He must have slept by the phone.

I smile and begin a response, but my phone rings. "Hey, you."

"Hey, yourself," he exhales groggily.

"Let me guess, you're still lying in bed? Because I am. And it's a lot earlier there than it is here."

"Yep," he yawns, "alone."

"Since most girls would probably object to their lover taking early morning phone calls from a married woman, I assume you wouldn't pick up the phone otherwise."

"If it was otherwise, my phone wouldn't ring because you could just poke me on the shoulder instead of call."

The realization that he wants me next to him as much as I want him next to me slices me in two.

Snuggled under the covers where I made love to Ethan last night, I picture Tad, alone in his apartment. I love Ethan. I do. But I miss Tad. I don't want to be there. I want him here.

"Mommy," Zach says as he trudges through my door, wiping the sleep from his eyes and carrying Bartles, "can I make oatmeal?" The kids are old enough to run the toaster oven, but they still need permission for the microwave.

"Sure," I respond, holding the phone away from my ear. "But don't put a spoon in it. Remember, no metal."

"Okay," He looks around the room. "Where is Dad? And who is that?"

"A friend," I reply. "Your dad is running another race. He'll be home around lunch."

Zach nods in acknowledgement and disappears to create his breakfast, leaving me with Tad.

We fall into conversation as if he is sitting in my den. We discuss the dance, his car trip, and all of the small intimacies of our lives that occurred over the last week.

After describing his accommodations to me in detail, he springs a surprise. "So, guess who'll be coming back for Christmas?" Actually, his tone doesn't reverberate with excitement, but the news sends a shot of adrenaline right through me. "I didn't plan to or really want to," he explains, "but my boss mentioned giving me the time off right in front of my parents, so there was no way I could avoid it and pretend like they wouldn't let me leave."

"You're coming home already?" My shock escalates to excitement. I didn't expect him to return quite so soon. Instead of trepidation or fear, determination steamrolls through my veins. Since I already cheated on Ethan and crossed the line, why not enjoy the reward and follow it through to its conclusion?

"I'll only be there a few days," he continues. "I fly in the day before Christmas, stay over the long weekend, and fly home in the morning on Tuesday."

"Really," I say, lost in thought. If there is any completely impossible time to escape my house, it is Christmas. I have a husband whose family all coalesce on our front porch and force us to host. I have two children who expect Santa to arrive promptly with everything perfectly wrapped and all the details finely executed. Ethan even takes vacation a few days before and after the holidays. The notion of even attempting to squeeze Tad into this time is impossible. "Let me think about it. Give me your flight times." So he does. I roll the possibilities around in my head, not only considering the opportunity to sleep with him, but also the logistics involved with not wanting it to be in my own home.

We finish our conversation, but nothing else that is said registers with me. I contemplate potential scenarios to make this work. This could be my last chance.

Chapter 25 ~ December

After two days of thinking, I have a plan. Ethan goes back to work on Tuesday. Tad's flight is the same day in the early afternoon. Either I can drive Tad to the airport and we can stop en route to rent a room or he can shuttle from the airport to a hotel and meet me after his friends drop him off to catch his flight. Meanwhile, I will schedule some "Mommy time" that day. I'll hire a sitter for the kids and reserve the day for myself.

I feel like a criminal mastermind. The lack of guilt confuses and confounds me. I am premeditating a way to have sex with a man who is not my husband and who in all likelihood has no long-term interest in me, no intent to raise my children, and no financial stability at all. In my head, I think I should feel guilty. But I don't. I sense this is my only—and last—chance.

I text the various options to Tad from the gym. He requests time to check out some details before we finalize anything. I thought he implied a timely reply, but almost two days pass before he broaches the subject again.

His response overwhelms my expectations. "Have a room that I will pay for. I will be in the city the night before. All you have to do is plan your day and show up."

Wow. He actually took care of all of it. I'm completely impressed. Ethan never executed any details like that during the entire course of our relationship. I immediately book our babysitter, ensuring she is available for the day, and record it on a Post-it so that I'll remember to run it by Ethan when he gets home. My tolerance wanes quickly when I'm trapped at home with the kids over the holidays. They need stimulation; I require silence and a change of scenery. My birthday is New Year's Eve, so I can sell it as an early birthday present. Happy birthday to me.

That evening, I pitch my day off to Ethan. He doesn't even bat an eyelash. He is accustomed to the escapes that I plot on a monthly basis. But he does inquire, "What do you plan to do all day?"

Shit. What do I plan to do? Whatever it is, it must allow me to leave the house super early. I can't claim I need to shop at J. Crew at seven a.m.. My mind races, searching for options. "I'll go to the gym and schedule a massage. The gym up by that mall is fantastic. Remember when I competed in their mini-triathlon?" This is no exaggeration. That gym is Mecca compared to the dinky one here in town; thank God my friend Alyssa convinced me to compete a few years ago when I didn't want to. "That way, I can leave before the kids wake up, because if I have to dress and feed them, it doesn't feel much like a day off for me." Wow. I did it. I invented a way not only to stay out of the house for the day, but to leave early and pack extra clothes. Who knew I had such skill as a liar?

Ethan helps me plan my day. He arranges to skip his workout to relieve the babysitter in the evening. He even pulls up the gym website and discovers they're running a free week pass for potential members. "Perfect," he says. "You can visit on Tuesday, and if you love it, we can go back again on Saturday for your birthday."

Even though Tad flies out around lunchtime, I reserve the remainder of the day for myself. I'll need it to compose myself before I walk back through the door. And I do actually enjoy my days without kids. No lying involved on that front. Before I know it, everything is arranged.

Tad and I intermittently text and flirt, but we both prefer actual conversations. He calls one last time, two days before Christmas break, while the kids are in school.

"So, is this really going to happen?" he asks immediately as I answer the phone.

"Yes," I reply. "If you're in, I am."

"But are you sure? When I left, you weren't sure. What made the difference? Why now and not before?"

"It's complicated." I plop down on my comforter. This is going to require some thought; he obviously expects more than light conversation. "First, when you left I assumed that would end it. I didn't actually believe we'd stay in contact. But we have. And it makes me more comfortable that that we can maintain this connection even from a distance. I don't think I can live without trying it. My entire life, I've done everything correctly. I graduated from high school as valedictorian. I made it through college with an engineering degree, I married right out of college and took a responsible job. I popped out two perfectly pre-planned children. Every decision has been what I'm supposed to do. Since you left, all I've done is regret that I said no. For once in my life, I want to make a colossal mistake, if that's what this is, and do something that makes me feel alive."

He fires back immediately with another question, "But what are your expectations?"

"I don't know," I think out loud, "What are yours?"

"You have to have some type of expectation."

"If you mean physically, no. Well, other than if it takes two hours I'll be completely insulted." I grin. "I think my skills are better than that. My expectation is a physical manifestation of the emotional connection. Yes, I want the physical bond with you, but it isn't about that. It is about sealing this magnetic connection with you. I've already done most of what you're just beginning and, even surrounded by friends, rarely do people find that deeper level.

"And while we're on the subject of expectations," I continue, "you act as if you don't have any. The pressure makes me anxious, too. You expect me to be the experienced one. I am, but you have to realize I've been married to the same man for almost fourteen years. Being with someone else is more foreign to me than it is to you. Not to mention, I'm quite a bit older and have had two children. My body isn't what it was at twenty-three. I have just as much reason to be nervous as you do."

"So we're set then?" Tad asks. "You're sure?"

"I am." The butterflies in my stomach take flight. I stand in the middle of my bedroom, the room I share every night with Ethan. Pictures of the two of us surround me on every side.

Chapter 26 ~ December

I'm so angry I could scream. But I already did that. Why can't this just be easier? We've been married for so long. How is it that he doesn't know what I need or want? It always starts innocuously enough.

"Whatcha doing?" I ask. I sit on the floor, surrounded by teacher gifts and wrapping supplies. Teacher gifts are the bane of my December existence. They are, in my opinion, the hardest things to buy. I never know what a teacher will appreciate.

"Relaxing," Ethan responds. No shit, Sherlock. He sprawls across our bed, surrounded by no less than eight giant decorative pillows, watching a football game.

"Could you help me tie this one?" Thank God for cold cups from Starbucks. I can't imagine anyone who doesn't drink something, so hopefully the teachers will appreciate them. But because it is impossible to hold tissue paper and cellophane and tie a bow simultaneously, they are a giant pain in the ass to wrap.

He sighs, but acquiesces and slides down onto the floor to tie the bow.

"Remember back when wrapping presents was enjoyable because we were so intense that we'd do anything to spend time together in the same room?" I reminisce. I miss those days when we couldn't keep our hands off each other and hung on each other's every word. Spending time with Tad reminds me of what I lost with Ethan. I search for warmth between us.

"I did what you asked me to," he huffs. "What else do you want?"

"For you to help?" I counter. I already decided on the gifts, purchased the wrapping paper, and coordinated who receives what, which is a giant time waster since my children have enough coaches and teachers that I need a spreadsheet to track them all.

"I did help. I tied the bow. Now I want to relax." Ethan turns his back and crawls into his pillow fortress.

The room quiets, but tension crackles through the air. Are we really fighting because I asked him to tie a blasted bow? And because I missed him and the days we used to adore each other? Well, guess what, buddy, this is progressing to a whole new level because I have three more bows that need to be tied before I can move along to the personalized note card sector.

I silently prepare all of the wrapping supplies. Finally stuck, I ask, "Can you tie a few more bows?"

He glares at me like he might actually murder me in my sleep tonight, but inches over to the side of the bed and snatches the ties. He ties them all. I sit in anticipation, waiting to see where this is going.

Finally, he speaks. "What is your problem? I worked all day. I skipped the gym to come home and help Maya study. I helped put the kids to bed. Can I please have a few minutes to relax now?"

"Relax? Really? Well, obviously you earned it," I spit out. "Whatever it was I did today didn't earn any free time. Oh, wait. I woke up, got everyone ready, and dropped Maya at school. I drove Zach to a doctor's appointment in Knoxville that consumed more than half the day. I pinned him down in the lab for a blood draw and stood in line at the pharmacy. I coordinated the babysitter to retrieve Maya after school. I prepared tonight's dinner last night, knowing there would not be time this evening due to the test tomorrow, the doctor's appointment, and Zach's soccer practice. And now I'm wrapping fucking teacher gifts that I already selected and purchased on my own. I didn't do enough to warrant a bit of relaxation."

That fires him up. No relaxation now, that's for sure. The TV flips off, Ethan's face flushes, and he jumps out of the bed. "What do you want from me?" he bellows, towering above me. "You keep looking for attention. Are you cheating on me?"

"Huh?" How did this morph from me desiring his attention, wanting to connect with him, into an accusation? Perhaps if he actually paid attention to me and every single conversation didn't dissolve into arguing an affair would be less likely, but I don't throw that into the conversation.

"I don't know what you do all day," he yells. "You wake up in the middle of the night and sit at the computer for hours. Maybe you have a secret boyfriend online or something. You overreact when I look at your phone or try to answer it."

"You know that when I can't sleep I play on the computer or read a book. I entertain myself downstairs so that I don't disturb you. Would you prefer I flop around in bed and keep you awake?

"Two," I continue, "you have access to my online accounts. You know the passwords and I leave them logged in. If I had a boyfriend, don't you think I'd have enough sense not to use them?

"And as for three, it is my phone," I growl. "I don't know more than half the contacts in your phone. Maybe they're from work, maybe elsewhere. I don't dive to read your text messages or grab it every time it rings. Did you ever consider that if someone wanted to talk to you, they'd call your phone?"

We glare at each other. Why is it we can't have a normal conversation about anything without it spinning completely out of control?

"I'm going to bed," he says. The decorative pillows whack into a pile in the corner as he throws them as hard as he possibly can. He pulls down the bedding, then storms into the bathroom to brush his teeth.

I flop back down at my wrapping station in the middle of the floor. Three more gifts to go. Tomorrow is the last day of school before the holidays, so these must be wrapped tonight. I measure paper to fit around the note cards.

"You're going to wrap now?" he asks. "I told you I'm going to bed."

"I have to finish it."

He doesn't speak again. Most of our fights consist of long periods of silence, punctuated by short bursts of yelling. But he sits down next to me. And he starts cleaning up the paper and supplies.

"Wait a minute, where's the tape?" I inquire.

"In the bin," he responds.

"It was next to me thirty seconds ago." I roll my eyes and sigh. "What are you doing?"

"Helping you," he retorts.

"This is not help," My eyes start to water. When Ethan wants to take control of a situation, he cleans. He has to be obsessive-compulsive. Even on days when he's not upset, the mail disappears if I drop it and run to the bathroom. The kids can't leave their homework on the table while we go to an evening activity because he piles it all up, sorts it according to some system the rest of us don't understand, and moves it to where he thinks it belongs. It takes an extra fifteen minutes to find it and set it all back out to work on again. The positive side to this is that, because he loves to clean, he vacuums the house at least twice a week. But his fixations are selective. He'll happily throw away my new magazine before I read it, perhaps because I abandoned it on the kitchen counter while I grabbed the phone, but he won't scrub a bathtub if barnacles adhere to the sides.

"I'm tired. I had a long day. I wanted to talk to you. Instead, you accuse me of cheating on you. Now you're stowing away my wrapping supplies while I'm in the middle of fucking wrapping."

He shuts off all the lights and burrows into the bed. Now I sit in the dark, surrounded by wrapping paper. I hop up, collect my supplies, and drag them down to the kitchen to finish.

Footsteps creak on the steps and I know what's coming. "Where did you go?" Ethan asks innocently. "Come to bed." This is supposed to be an apology. He rubs my shoulders and pulls my hand. But it actually isn't an apology. It's his way of controlling me. He wants me to come upstairs, have sex, and console him after the fight.

"No," I answer firmly. "I have to finish the wrapping. I told you that. I came downstairs to do it. Now could you please let me do this? They have to go to the school tomorrow."

And he does. He trudges back up the stairs. We don't speak again for nine days, although our silence doesn't decrease the frequency of his evening expectations. Actually, we don't speak again until Christmas Eve, when we drink too much and have to play nice while we host his family for the holiday.

Chapter 27 ~ December

I stick the casserole in the oven and plod down to the den to pick up the remains of the Christmas debris. Maya and Zach happily munch on their favorite tutti-frutti jelly beans and are probably quickly approaching nausea. They busily shuffle all of their presents into piles so that they can compare their loot. Ethan, meanwhile, sits at a table fighting with what looks to be an eight-thousand-piece Lego castle.

For the first time in days, I steal a few minutes to myself to think. Tad made it home and stopped by yesterday. The minute I opened the door, he inquired, "Is Ethan home?" It wasn't a let's-sneak-away-if-he-isn't type of question.

"Really?" I responded, with a raised eyebrow.

"Yes, really," he said.

"I'm pretty sure he's in the shower." I walked up the stairs and informed Ethan that Tad was here and wanted to talk to him.

While we waited, Tad stood in the kitchen. I offered him a seat, but he declined. At that point, my confusion must have been apparent. Although he mindlessly chattered until Ethan joined us, his eyes held mine the entire time and I knew the words pouring out didn't pertain to the thoughts behind them.

Once Ethan arrived, he started over, reliving every moment from the time he left until the present, excluding, of course, all the conversations with me. He prattled on for over an hour. I could sense Ethan was restless. He likes Tad, but couldn't understand why he was here. I didn't either, for that matter. I got the impression he was testing me somehow. I couldn't decide if he was dangling a carrot, so to speak, if he was probing to see if I could handle being around him in front of Ethan, or if he desired my company enough that he didn't care if Ethan was here or not.

So now, on Christmas, with my family all around me, all I can concentrate on is the fact that Tad is right next door. Is he doing the same? Does he sit, surrounded by his family, thinking of me? I push him back in my mind, but the thought reappears with every trip outside to the garbage can. He is almost impossible to escape.

The rest of the morning passes uneventfully. Ethan's family arrives for our usual lunch, but this year I serve them casserole instead. I used to prepare a huge Christmas feast almost equivalent to Thanksgiving, but in recent years I've selected the easiest meal I can design. The plan is to allow the most time I can have with the children while spending the least time possible in the kitchen. However, now I wish I had planned a big meal. I need something to occupy my idle hands, and, more importantly, my idle mind.

After lunch, it is tradition that Ethan, his parents, and I take the kids to see a movie. When Zach was younger, I stayed home because he needed a nap and couldn't sit through a full length show, but we passed that stage long ago. This year, I can't go. I can't, knowing that Tad is right next door, but only until tomorrow. Then he will be gone.

"Do you care if I stay home?" I ask Ethan. "You know I sit through kid shows constantly. Is there any way I can reserve a few hours of quiet? I'll clean up the mess from this morning, maybe go for a run, and then have dinner ready when you guys come home."

Ethan looks hurt, but will never dissuade me from exercise. It is a guaranteed excuse at all times, because Lord knows he'd never turn down an exercise session for me. "Sure," he says, although his expression doesn't look like he means it.

The kids are so excited to see the movie that they tumble over each other to put their shoes and coats on. I can only wish they'd move that fast on a school day. Within minutes, everyone packs into my minivan and they pull out of the driveway.

Once they're gone, I clean up the den. Scraps of wrapping paper hide in every crevice of the sofa and it takes a while to unearth them all and bag them. Then I inspect each toy to ensure we aren't accidentally throwing away a key element. Last year we disastrously threw out a Webkins code by mistake since Ethan didn't comprehend that the tag to unlock your electronic animal was much more important than the actual physical toy. It took hours of trash digging to locate it, so now I am more paranoid about the toy details.

I submerge the meat in the sink to thaw, then tromp up to my room to select an outfit to run in. Once I am fully polyester-clad, complete with high ponytail, iPod, and running gloves, I stop in the bathroom one last time. And then I look at my phone. Because Tad is right next door. Or at least I'm guessing he is. It's Christmas Day. He's supposed to appreciate his time home with his family. Of course, I'm supposed to do the same, but can't quite manage to keep my mind tracking in the right direction.

I pick up the phone and text, "You busy?"

A few minutes pass before he answers, but I finally receive a lovely one-word text, "No."

"Have some free time. You interested?"

This time, his reply takes about five minutes. I'm annoyed now, because I don't plan to miss my run waiting for him to text me back when I know he's sitting by or on his phone.

When the answer arrives, I decide it was worth the wait. "Yep. Be there in a few minutes."

My heart pounds. I may not be running, but the adrenaline kick through my system could probably burn just as many calories. I check myself out in the mirror, trying to decide if I should change my clothes. My Under Armour is, well, armor. It is extremely tight. When I imagine him pulling it off me, it makes me chuckle. But that might be a good thing. Although I want to spend time with Tad, I still don't want things to go too far. We're in my house. And even though I made the decision to go through with this in two days, I'm not ready to now, not surrounded by my kids' new Christmas toys and stockings full of candy.

Tad knocks lightly on the door and lets himself in. The minute he comes through the door, away from the windows, I leap into his arms. His tongue probes mine and he pulls back only long enough to whisper, "Now this, I've missed." He grabs my ass and yanks me up so that he's holding me, with my legs wrapped around his waist, and I can instantly feel how much he wants me.

He walks over to the sofa and attempts to lay me down gracefully. It doesn't work well because he's so tall, and we both fall onto the sofa, laughing. He doesn't stop kissing me as he unpacks everything from his phone to his handcuff keys out of his pants and places them on the table. This time, there is no discussion about any of it. I can't be bothered to examine the contents of his pockets when I have him here.

A sudden thought crosses my mind. What if Ethan comes back? His parents were with him, so they could easily stay at the movie with the kids. What if Ethan decides it would be a great Christmas present for his parents to watch the kids so that he and I can spend some time alone together? I could justify Tad being here, but probably not the state we're in right now.

The thought fades as Tad, while kissing me, slides down the side of the sofa so that he kneels next to me. His hand, currently still outside of my polyester armor shell, travels down my stomach and over my hipbones. My breath comes in pants as he traces lines on my abdomen, gently shifting the waistband of my pants, taunting me. It's bizarre that, even as adults, during a month when the space between us compressed to almost nothing, we still haven't crossed this line. Every element within me yearns for his touch.

He looks into my eyes with determination as his hand dips down my pants, shifting my thong out of the way. There is no teasing, no foreplay now. His fingers probe for a split second before he rams them inside of me. There is no skill or subtlety. He is raw, not understanding the nuances that drive a woman to pleasure, but I am overcome by him all the same. I arch my back to draw his fingers into me further, and slowly unbuckle his belt. As his tongue continues to glide into my mouth and his fingers slide through me, I tentatively reach down behind the belt buckle.

There isn't far to go. His tip pokes through the waistband of his boxers. He is silky smooth, but hard and ready. I reach further down, not so much to pleasure him as to explore him. As I begin to stroke, he yanks his hand out of my pants. "Let's go," he orders, clutching my hand and all but pulling me down the steps to the basement. As I approach the bottom step, he lunges for me. Never ceasing the contact, we stumble to the sofa where I climb to straddle him. His hands frantically begin to pull up my shirt.

"Stop." The word flies from my mouth; it is a knee-jerk reaction. My brain spins. Am I going to go this far, on Christmas Day, in my basement? How do I react if Ethan pulls into the driveway? Other pressing issues I hadn't anticipated pop into my mind and demand consideration. I am wearing an extremely constricting sports bra. Not only does it take forever to put on and take off, it also smashes me to the point that my breasts will look weird. And I haven't groomed downstairs for a few days. Some women like a natural look, but I do not. I prefer to be tidy. Obviously none of these issues are show stoppers for him, but they halt my momentum. If I go through with this, I want it to be perfect, or as perfect as I can make it. This is not ideal.

"I can't do this now, Tad," I resist, attempting to impose restraint. "Yes, I want to be with you, but not like this. We already had this conversation. Not in my house, not with one ear open for my husband to pull in the driveway, not with a time limit, and not even when this is my fantasy location. You already know I want to. You can feel it. And I know you do, too. And I'm fine with what we're doing now, but it won't go further, not today."

His disappointed expression slashes through me, but I hold my ground and he doesn't push the issue. The intensity lingers as we continue our exploration of each other, so he must not be too upset. After another hour, we part. He has family functions to attend; I worry that the longer we linger, the higher the chance of being caught. Children's movies are shorter than adult flicks.

After cementing our forthcoming plans, Tad repacks his pockets and kisses me good-bye. I check the clock; no time remains to run now. I sort the laundry, shed my armor, and throw it all in the wash. After I shower, I return one more time to the basement to ensure that everything is in its place.

I'm in the kitchen finishing dinner when I hear the van pull into the drive. Doors slam, and Maya and Zach giggle and squeal excitedly while they discuss the latest Chipmunks movie. The front door handle wiggles a few times before Ethan pushes them out of the way, unlocks the door, and hustles everyone inside.

They unload through the front door with a giant commotion. My mother-in-law Sarah exclaims over and over how well-behaved our children are. Obviously, she doesn't see them enough to really know them. My father-in-law Richard grunts as he grabs a glass and rummages in the refrigerator for a drink.

"Dinner is ready. Please make a plate and we can eat," I offer. The adults all sit to eat, but the kids remain upstairs playing Legos. Their interest in real food disappeared after gorging on movie popcorn.

The dinner conversation moves slowly. Ethan and I don't have much in common with his parents, so generally our conversation revolves around the kids. This time, however, Sarah and Richard tell stories from their past. Somehow, we begin discussing neighbors and, ironically, at the same time Sarah tells an in-depth story about her neighbors cheating on their spouses and how she accidentally walked in on one of their sessions, Tad happens to come out of his house and decides to stand outside our dining room window and throw a football with Theo. Luckily my dinner was finished or I would have choked.

Chapter 28 ~ Tuesday

I wake up with butterflies. I think I'm going to be sick to my stomach. The clock says it is only 3:14 a.m. Ethan snores next to me. He lies on his side, facing away from me, so I snuggle behind him, feeling the warmth of his furry body as I snake my arm around his waist. I lightly kiss his back and burrow in tighter. I lie completely still and try to match my breathing to his, hoping it will help me fall back asleep, but my mind races. In four hours, I will leave the house. In five and a half, I'll be with Tad. Is it really so close now? Can I go through with it? Can I actually pull it off so that it doesn't ruin my life?

I spin thoughts of both Ethan and Tad round and round in my head. How did I arrive at this point with Ethan? I love him. He is my family. Last night we actually had a decent evening. He treated me like a person and I pretended to be one.

Our relationship turned into a sink-or-swim, every-man-for-himself competition. All of the stable, content couples that I know depend on their spouse for support. If there is one thing I have finally accepted in this relationship, it is that Ethan never, ever will support me in any way other than financially. He won't help if I fall, call if I'm lonely, or even listen if I want to talk. He doesn't believe me when I'm sick, help with the kids when I'm vomiting, or offer to pitch in on a project unless I guilt him into it.

My life with Ethan isn't a total disaster. He loves our kids and me in his own way. He provides for our family. I know I can trust him. We run an extremely efficient, organized ship together. We specialize in our own areas of expertise so that we never duplicate work. We are the perfect business partnership.

Ethan is also a fantastic lover. Or was. So maybe I shouldn't be comparing, but Ethan had enough experience before I came along that he knew all kinds of tricks; he surprised me, and I wasn't exactly inexperienced. In bed, he was more give than take and always used to say that he enjoyed it more when I enjoyed it. But over the years, that dwindled. His drive is as high as ever, but the passion is gone. We rarely, if ever, kiss during sex and his eyes—except on very rare occasions—are closed for the entire experience. Sex with no attachment makes me feel emptier inside. I feel like a well-paid prostitute at times.

I lie next to my husband, stare at the ceiling, and justify why in a few hours I will have sex with the twenty-three year old son of our neighbor. When I phrase it that way, I'm relatively certain this resembles a Lifetime movie of the week. I know it's selfish. I know it goes against absolutely everything I stand for, and that if Ethan ever discovers my indiscretion, it will crush him. As I gaze around my beautiful, comfortable room filled with furniture and pictures that Ethan and I accumulated over our years, what I am risking sinks in. "But I am so lonely," a tiny voice inside my head screams. I am. I am so lonely that I will risk it all for a few hours of feeling like someone can actually see me.

I must have fallen asleep, because I jerk awake as my alarm sounds. I fly out of the bed and into the shower. My heart races and my hands tremble so violently that I can hardly hold the razor. At this rate, I'm going to look like a crazy cutter instead of a sexy older woman.

Maya's old school backpack waits for me on the floor by the sink when I emerge from my shower with a smooth, hair-free body. For the gym, I need workout clothes, shoes, and my iPod. For my shower after working out, I need shampoo, a hair brush, and makeup. The only concession to where I'm stopping off on the way is the extra pair of underwear that I throw into the bottom of the bag, since the fate of the ones I'm currently wearing is yet to be determined.

Once the bag is packed, I blow my hair dry and add some light makeup. A giant zit perches grotesquely on my nose. I attempt to camouflage it, but it refuses the disguise. Acne in middle age is frustrating. My only consolation is that perhaps all the oil will prevent me from wrinkling for a while. There isn't much I can do about it now. I pull on my sweater and jeans, pluck the backpack off the counter, and rush to the kitchen for some breakfast, anticipating the babysitter's arrival.

I nervously pace around the kitchen until I hear Ethan begin to stir. I snatch the backpack and check the front pocket. A tiny slip of paper, slipped in last night while everyone else slept, hides inside with the address of the hotel where I plan to meet Tad. I scrunch it back up and zip the pocket. I review my email and the news headlines on the computer to channel my energy. If it isn't focused somewhere, Ethan is going to notice. I'm reading an article about someone pilfering money from Salvation Army kettles when he grabs his coat to leave.

"Have a good day by yourself," Ethan says, tossing protein bars into his briefcase.

"I will." I stand and slide both arms along his neck to hug him goodbye. To reciprocate, Ethan wraps an arm around me and half-squeezes. "I love you, Ethan." I pull back a smidge, trying to catch his eye, somehow hoping he'll look at me and make me feel something for him. We never say that in the mornings. We don't say it much at all.

"Yep." Ethan's phone balances in his other hand and he is checking his messages over my shoulder. He turns on his heel to open the garage door. "See you this evening." He walks out the door and is gone. He never even looked at me.

Minutes later, the babysitter arrives. I warned her that I want to leave extremely early so that I don't have to help Maya and Zach start moving for the day. Once she settles in with the TV remote instructions, I take one last look around my home, and walk out the door.

Before I leave town, I fill the car with gas and call Tad.

"Morning," I say. "You awake?"

"Yes, ma'am," he responds. "I'm waiting on you. See you in a bit."

We hang up. He sounds as nervous as I am. I crank up the CD that I made for the car that contains all of my favorite hip-hop music and sing at the top of my lungs. It burns off the anxiety and helps me breathe. When I pull into the parking lot of the Holiday Inn by the airport, I don't hesitate. Whatever reservations I've had disappear. Tad waits on the other side of that door and there is nothing I want more in this world than to make love with him. I sling Maya's backpack over my shoulder and pitch the scrap of paper with the hotel address into the trash can as I walk through the sliding door into the hotel.

Tad is seated in the lobby, alone, eating breakfast and reading a newspaper. What look to be retired couples surround him.

"Eating?" I ask. "Really?"

"Are you hungry? You're welcome to eat some of this."

"Uh, no. Food would make me sick right now. My stomach is a bit nervous." I smile.

He catches my eye, rises, and throws out his food. "Okay, then."

I follow him to the elevator. The ride up is awkward. We don't speak and his fleeting eye contact makes me jittery. I'm suddenly conscious of my wedding and engagement rings. I don't know which is worse. Do I wear them or take them off? It isn't like he doesn't know I'm married. I decide that they will remain in place.

We walk down a silent hall until he pauses in front of a door. He utters a few expletives as he wrestles with the keycard, then holds the door open for me. I step in and drop my bag on the chair. The room is comfortable, complete with mass produced artwork over the bed. I slip off my coat and look to Tad for direction. He freezes next to the door after shutting and locking it. Stiffly, he rambles, making no eye contact, telling tell me about the movie he saw last night.

I maneuver myself directly in front of him and whisper, "Stop," before he finally meets my eyes. Abruptly, his arms encircle me while his mouth crushes down on mine. I hop, wrapping my legs around his waist. I love this feeling with him, the feeling as he supports me. It's an unfamiliar sensation. He grinds me against him as he carries me the few paces to the bed and tumbles on top of me. The kissing, the touching, and the pulling are frantic. I can't close the distance between us fast enough.

He slowly extricates himself, excusing it with a shrug. "Shoes." Mine slipped themselves off along the way, but Tad wears gigantic lace-up boots that appear to require some effort to remove. By the time he sheds them, the steam is dissipating. When he rolls back to me, his look indicates thought, not urgency. "Are you sure?" he asks, his eyes boring into mine with the seriousness I have come to expect from him.

"Yes," I answer, and I mean it with every fiber of my being. "I am absolutely sure." And with that, he grasps the bottom of my sweater, yanks it over my head, and bears down on me as urgently as before. I unbutton his shirt and, the minute it hits the floor, start on his belt buckle. Somehow he manages to wiggle me free of my jeans without attracting my notice. Our clothing evaporates. He steps across the room and digs through a small toiletry bag to grab a condom. As he walks, I lie on the bed and watch, noting how his body differs from the one I see every day. He is tall, lean, and angular; what body hair he has is sparse, dark, and clumped in patches. Just watching him move incites a yearning that is spreading down my abdomen and I moisten in anticipation.

When he returns to the bed, he huddles next to me as he unrolls the condom. I would offer to help, but years have passed since that necessity, so I fear for my skill. When Tad finishes, he looks to me, as if expecting instructions. My mouth covers his as I roll to my back, spread my thighs, and pull his weight on top of me. Our lips continue to collide as I reach to guide him toward his destination. I inhale sharply as he pushes all the way in. I gaze up and his eyes smile as they meet mine.

At the same time, he begins pumping furiously. Oh, brother. I should have anticipated this. He did tell me that his first attempt lasted two hours. He was proud of his incredible stamina, but for anyone with experience, two hours of flat out pumping usually indicates a problem. I clutch his ass and provide resistance, hoping to restrain his urgency. "Slowly," I mouth, "tease me. There is no rush."

He tries, but has no rhythm, no fluidity. Finally, I halt him altogether. "Flip over," I order. He surrenders his position and I climb above him, straddling him but remaining vertical so that he can watch me. "Now hold still." I begin to slowly slide up and down. We work our way into a rhythm. I'm close to the finish and I feel him lengthening inside me when he suddenly gasps, "I'm going to come." With that challenge, I forget myself and slam onto him, tightening my muscles to grip as I do. He sucks in a breath, then exhales.

Do I stop? Was that it? Confusion surfaces. When Ethan and I are together, there is no question. With the way he moans and shudders, it is completely apparent that it is over. But with Tad, I can't tell.

"Did you?" I finally ask.

He grins and nods his head.

I check the clock. "Look at that. We've been here less than forty-five minutes altogether and we spent part of that time clothed. I told you she didn't know what she was doing," I inform him, just to rub it in. I'm still tightly wound and frustrated, but expect him to relieve that pressure soon enough. I collapse onto his chest and he nibbles the side of my face as we discuss constellations and nuzzle against each other, examining our newfound territories.

When enough time has passed, I bring up the shower. My fantasy may have been the basement, but this was his. I am compelled to raise the issue. "So are we going to try out the shower? How do you plan for that to work?"

Tad looks embarrassed; he obviously has no idea. He still hasn't rebounded from the last session, but I'm impatient. "No, we can wait." He wavers instead of encouraging me.

"How often is this opportunity going to present itself? Let's go." Without giving him an option, I jump out of bed and scurry to the shower. "Oh, and take that thing off," I say, motioning to the used condom that he still hasn't bothered to remove.

Warm spray from the showerhead splatters the room as Tad climbs in behind me. He stoops to kiss me and droplets spill down my face. Time for my finish. Perhaps I am completely selfish, but I expect to climax every time; Ethan has me spoiled in that regard. Tad isn't ready, so I decide to boost his momentum. I drop to my knees and take him in my mouth. "Holy shit," he gasps and I watch his knees buckle before he regains his balance. Perhaps he thinks I mean to take him all the way like this, but I don't. Someday maybe, but right now this is all about me. Once Tad is primed, I come up for air and stabilize myself on the edges of the tub. We attract, magnetic, pulling apart only to crash back together again. It's uncomfortable, to put it mildly. My calves scream as I balance on my tippy toes and he takes me.

Once the position becomes too difficult to maintain, I descend back down to floor of the tub. "To be continued," I announce, as I turn off the water, throw him a towel, and dive soaking wet onto the bed. He follows. This time, there is no question as to where I'm going. I climb on top of him and ride him until I am satisfied. As I finish, his enthusiasm dwindles. I attribute this to his incomplete performance.

Tad flips over to check the clock. "Should we shower and get ready to go?" Sooner than I'd anticipated, he transitions, forcing us into reality instead of dwelling on our imminent loss.

"Why? We still have at least an hour and a half." I inhale in deep relaxation as my cheek brushes his chest.

"Actually, they bumped my flight up an hour. We need to be out of here in thirty minutes," he says. "Do you need to take a shower?"

My heart stops. Literally. For just a moment. The limited time was a condition of this offer, but now my enjoyment is abruptly rationed as well. Disappointment slices through me, but my response is restrained.

"I'll start moving in a minute," I sigh, recognizing that the second the shower envelops me, this serenity will cease to exist.

"So what are you going to do?" Tad redirects my attention from his own withdrawal, but his gentle eyes admit his pain. "Stella, are you going to be okay? You know I may not return. Or if I do, it may be a long time from now and everything may be different."

"I know," I say. "But if we're in contact, there will be no unexpected revelations. I'll either know that we're close friends or I'll know that you've met someone or I'll know that our feelings have changed. And if we're not in contact, then you can never presume that this will happen again. I'll just walk away."

His gaze declares a completely open, undisguised want. In one motion, he overthrows me, frantically pushing my thighs apart as his mouth closes down on mine. This time, there is no holding back; the passage is familiar. As he rises above me to meet my eyes, my hands trace lines down his chest. "What do you want, Tad?" I ask, knowing I might not have the opportunity again. "Show me. What do you want?"

He stiffens in bewilderment, evaluating my unexpected offer. His eyes probe mine one last time, determining how far I'll allow him to go, before he emphatically positions me onto all fours and enters me from behind. He pounds me frantically, with an uncontrolled intensity I've never felt from him before. My body quakes beneath him as he divides me. All the while, his hands cover mine and his breath warms my ear.

I've had sex in this position many times, but only with Ethan. Ethan is the only one I allowed that close, trusting him enough to forgo contact with his eyes. Now, with Tad, it is different. I'm not as comfortable with this, but I refuse to back out now. I trust him. His warmth surrounds me as his chest presses into my back. Instead of focusing on his actions, I concentrate on his hand grasping mine. Luckily, it is quick.

When he finishes, I realize that if I lay down next to him, I'll cry, and I don't want him to see that. I will cry because the emotion is so intense that I'm overwhelmed. I will cry because I know I won't see him again anytime soon. But more than anything, I will cry because, deep in my heart, I wish that Ethan would find me with that same vehemence. I wish that he could elicit the emotion that he did when we were younger. I will cry because I miss feeling young with opportunities for my life. But I don't. Instead, I smile gently, kiss Tad briskly, and jump into the shower. I guess a consolation of being older is that, when you want to, you can repress the despair and no one can tell.

I emerge from the shower to a flurry of activity. Tad has cleaned the room, folded my clothes and placed my shoes in front of them, and is now efficiently sorting all of our belongings. While I dry my hair, he showers. We are both ready to walk out the door in under ten minutes. As we gather our bags to leave, I stop to embrace him one last time, to delineate our closure. He pecks me on the lips, but looks past my eyes for the flight schedule on his phone. It is strangely reminiscent of Ethan leaving for work this morning.

As I drive Tad to the airport and jostle my way into the drop-off lane at the terminal, he sings along to the radio. Once I secure a spot to idle the car, he lightly kisses my lips. "Take care," he says, before grabbing his bags out of the backseat.

"See you," I respond, and he shuts the door. I linger a minute to watch his tall frame move toward the entrance. His military mode returns, apparent in his stiff posture and the precision of his step. I sigh, turn on my blinker, and merge to leave.

The remainder of my day rushes by in a blur. My first stop is the gym, where I run to avoid the questions that surface from this morning, reassuring myself of my contentment. Afterward, crumpled on the massage table, the tension releases. I meander aimlessly though a bookstore, immune to the chaos surrounding me, and amble through the streets of shops, stopping at whatever holds my eye.

As the overcast sky darkens, snow begins to fall. The time to venture home approaches. One more text, I think. Tad must be sitting in an airport somewhere, reliving this in a similar fashion. I write, "Hey. Had a fantastic time today. Hope all is well on your flight. Talk to you soon."

My phone dings back a few minutes later. "Damn airline. Sitting in Las Vegas. Have been for hours." He continues with three subsequent texts ranting about traveling. There is no mention of our morning together, no concern for me, no pleasantry at all for that matter. My insides drop, but I dismiss the emotion; travel can be frustrating.

When I arrive home and step through the door, I hear music wafting up from the basement. Maya and Zach are playing dance studio and taking turns giving performances. The kitchen smells of the chili that Ethan left out on the counter in case I'm hungry. I lean into the countertop and swallow a deep breath. I'm home. I hear Ethan in the basement now also, offering critiques on the dance solos. I gather myself, take one last long look in the mirror as I walk down the steps, and open the door to the basement. A chorus greets me. "Mommy, I'm so glad you're home. Let me show you...."

Chapter 29 ~ December

Thank God Ethan plans to work long days this week. I need time to arrange my thoughts, and although that isn't the easiest thing to do while Zach and Maya pillow fight in front of the TV, it is preferable to adult conversation. My distraction would prevent me from managing a coherent discussion anyway.

Wednesday speeds by and my phone refuses to ring or buzz. No text. No email. Nothing from Tad. A tiny voice in the back of my head starts to whimper, but I push it down. His flight was apparently horrible and he probably collapsed for the day to recover. And he still functions in college mode and sleeps until noon when he can, so the probability that he is even awake yet in his time zone is pretty slim. My rationalizations console me and keep the fear at bay.

Thursday passes with no contact. Memories surface, reminding me of college and the disillusion that follows such intensity. But even then, I never slept with a guy who didn't bother to call the next day. Never. Even the one night stands were decent guys. I stop myself. College is a bygone era. I am married, with children, and this experience was supposed to supplement my life. But from the beginning, our feelings complicated our friendship. And now, in the silence, my emotions loom, waiting to consume me. A fear expands in my chest, and it has nothing to do with Ethan leaving me or even finding out.

My resolve waivers. I refuse to concede outright, so instead I send an email, reiterating that I enjoyed our time together and proposing that we speak on Friday night. Ethan intends to drink and watch ball that night, so once the kids surrender to their beds, my evening will be empty. Instead of requesting a response, I just ask him to shoot me a text if it isn't convenient and let it go. The pressure eases a little just knowing a bit of communication links us.

By Friday afternoon, my excitement intensifies. I shouldn't anticipate a phone call so much, but I do. Tuesday until today is the longest span of time that has passed without contact between us since this began. I need him to discuss his perspective with me to reconcile our morning together in my mind. Thus far, we've evaluated everything between us each step of the way. I desire reassurance that our time together wasn't a gigantic mistake. A profound longing replaces the subdued sadness I felt as he left. I need confirmation that he didn't simply dismiss me after permeating my soul.

Some infinitesimally tiny particulate of mine migrated to him during our time together. Even though the physical acts weren't completely in sync, little practice should solve that problem. I crave another chance to explore him. Maybe it's arrogant, but I want to be the one to demonstrate what his body is capable of and watch him respond.

Finally, as the afternoon fades into evening, Ethan stalks in the door more than an hour late, dumps his bag in the hall closet, and stomps upstairs to bathe and change. I know he is avoiding the kids, but no greeting passes his lips.

Forty-five minutes later he returns to the kitchen. I haven't prepared dinner since he's going out. Three crescent rolls harden on the counter; Maya and Zach abducted the others to the basement hours ago. I open and close the refrigerator door, but nothing materializes between door slams to whet my appetite. My stomach growls.

"How was your day?" I ask Ethan, trying to be nonchalant.

He's dressed to go out, but his face flushes red from what must have been an extremely hot bath. When he closes the distance between us, the heat emanates from his skin under his T-shirt. Beads of sweat cling to his temples. Ethan loves to take baths, but also depends on them for stress relief, so this indicates a mess of a day. "Ugh," he grunts. "I hate this place. Thank God I'm going out tonight because I need it." He opens the refrigerator and grabs a Gatorade.

"What happened?" I have to coax the story out of him before he leaves. Tomorrow is New Year's Eve, which also happens to be my birthday, and this mood could easily carry over for three or four days. If I can eliminate it now, perhaps I can salvage tomorrow. We have a babysitter and are scheduled to spend the entire day together.

"Don't get me started," he responds. "It isn't one thing. It's a thousand little things. Doctors don't put the correct notes in charts, lab results aren't communicated to patients who need them, and some quality board that has nothing to do with our office and no idea how it runs rejected the blasted office procedure I keep rewriting. How am I supposed to meet my deadline if they keep rejecting the procedure but my boss won't sign off on their changes because it isn't actually what we do?"

I debate which angle to tackle this from. I can approach it from a just relax standpoint, but he is fired up and that will probably agitate him. I can approach it from a practical side and give advice to bring the two disagreeing parties together in a room, but he will probably interpret that as me telling him what to do. So instead, I turn on the empathy. "That stinks. They obviously don't see or appreciate how hard you work. Try to remember that every hour they pull you around and change their minds is still an hour that you're paid for. I know it isn't easy to think of it that way when you care as much as you do, but you care too much about it. You want to please them all and excel, but you can't care about it more than they do."

My comment hits the target because Ethan pushes the refrigerator closed and engulfs me in a bear hug. "I'm sorry. I shouldn't be taking this out on you. I'm just frustrated. So I'll get out of your way tonight, blow off some steam, and maybe I'll wake you up later." His phone buzzes, and he pulls away to check it. "They already have a table," he informs me. "Do you care if I go?"

"Have a good time," I say. He brushes my lips, yanks on his coat, grabs his keys, and runs out the door.

When their zebra movie ends, I herd Maya and Zach up the steps to brush their teeth and put on their PJs. "Where's Daddy?" Maya wants to know when I join her to say prayers and tuck her in. "Did he come home from work today?"

"He did, but he was in a hurry." I search for an excuse as I brush out her hair. "He was running really late when he came out of work and then he had plans to meet his friends tonight."

"Are you and Daddy friends?"

My breath catches and I compose myself. "Of course Daddy and I are friends," I reassure her. "Daddy is my best friend. That's why we got married and chose to spend our lives together."

"Maci is my best friend. I tell her everything," confides Maya. "She always knows when I'm angry about Mrs. March giving us too much homework. And she knows when I'm worried about orchestra because you know I can never remember which note is which. One day, she let me look at her music and she wrote in all the letters by the notes on mine to help me."

"I'm so happy you have a good friend." We conclude our routine, but inside I'm buzzing. Do I have a best friend? I used to. Ethan. But somewhere along the line, Ethan transformed from my friend into just another person to manage. Now he doesn't fill in the notes for me.

I tuck Zach in uneventfully and finally crash on the sofa. My stomach churns as I glance at the phone. Usually, Tad and I text before calling, but tonight I decide he was given fair warning. Don't be a coward, I tell myself. As I pick up the phone and dial, a strange feeling that something has already changed between us surfaces.

"Hello," Tad answers on the first ring.

"Hey, you," I chime. "What's up?"

"Not much. I'm getting dressed and meeting some people for dinner in a few minutes. What are you up to?"

"Same old thing. Just put the kids in bed and finally have a minute to myself."

Tad talks about his job and the people he's dining with. There's nothing wrong with the conversation, per se, but something is off. I listen and offer supportive "Uh-huh" noises as I watch the clock tick down through the minutes. Finally, I interrupt his monologue.

"Tad," I query, "are you going to mention anything about our time together?"

"Why? I thought it went well. I enjoyed being with you."

"I don't know." I sigh, annoyed. "Maybe because we just took this huge step and you didn't call for three days? What just happened, Tad? Did it mean anything to you at all?"

"Yes and no," he says. He apparently feels accused of something, because his tone becomes stiff and factual. "Yes, it means something to me and, no, it can't mean more than it should."

My pulse pounds in my ears. I sit in silence because I have absolutely no idea how to respond.

"Stella? You still there?"

"Yes."

"I can't talk much longer. I'm in the car now, but I only have until I pull into the restaurant parking lot, just so you know."

I'm still silent. I can't choke out any words. I haven't heard from Tad in three days. And now, instead of reassuring me, he is doing the exact opposite. So I hang up.

The Tad I knew a week ago would have wanted to discuss every possible philosophical variation of how this huge step would impact us. Our limited time to talk would have included flirting and banter. I am angry. So angry I want to punch my hand through a wall. Instead, I pour myself a margarita that is probably three-quarters tequila and down it.

About the time I finish, my phone buzzes with a text. Tad writes, "Sorry if I was rude. If you want to talk, you can call and I'll step out during dinner."

How gallant of you. My mental voice drips sarcasm. I want to erupt, but I squelch the urge. "I can't talk right now. Sorry to hang up, but I ran out of words and didn't know what to say. TTYL."

I struggle to watch a movie, but my concentration is zilch. I decide to write him an email. I won't send it tonight, maybe not ever, but my emotions need to spill out somewhere and my options are pretty limited. I can't exactly call my husband and cry that my boyfriend is acting like a complete jerk. Halfway through the email, I accept defeat. The words on the page circle me back to the confusion that triggered them, so I pour another margarita, guzzle it, and collapse on the sofa.

Ethan creeps in quietly sometime after midnight. He kisses down my neck to wake me as he snuggles me. In my alcohol fog, not completely awake, I relax and smile. His hands run through my hair and down over my bra as he starts to nibble on my lip. Ethan. He is so warm, so perfectly fit and hard, yet somehow so soft. He slips his shirt off and his course chest hair rubs my cheek as I tuck into my spot right between his shoulder and chin.

He slides off the side of the sofa to his knees and his hands travel down the front of my body, slowing only to pop the button on my jeans and unzip them. His kisses are light across my mouth and face as his fingers find their destination and he slides them inside me. My body quivers and somewhere in the haze Tad reaches into me and whispers that earlier was all a misunderstanding and he regrets his blunt disregard. Tad ravages me…

My eyes fly open in horror as Ethan removes his fingers and begins to undress me. I'm not with Tad. This is my husband, the one I am never supposed to disregard. Making love to him is supposed to be sacred. But thoughts of Tad whirl through my mind. I imagine his body, long and thin, stretched over mine. I envision his green eyes piercing mine as he flows through me. My own eyes well with tears and I roll to bury my face in the pillow as Ethan removes my pants. His body warms my back, and as the tears roll silently down my face into the upholstery, Ethan enters me. He massages my neck, kisses my back, and runs his hands through my hair; he is loving and gentle and tender. I try. I concentrate with agonizing effort on his pleasure. It requires my full attention; every time I start to let myself go, my mind rebounds to picture Tad holding my hands and breathing in my ear when he was behind me this way. I panic. And as I panic, my tears turn to sobs.

Ethan stops moving and lies still on my back. He cocoons around me, smoothing my hair and petting my head like a child to comfort me. He doesn't even ask what is wrong. I am choking on my sobs to the point I couldn't explain anyway. When my tears are spent, I lay inert with him inside me while he continues to gently stroke my hair until we fall asleep.

Sometime in the wee morning hours, Ethan nudges me, pulls my hand, and guides me up the stairs and into our bed. He doesn't leave my side or break physical contact even for a second. We meld together under the covers as we return to sleep. Hazily, I realize that I may never be able to return to Ethan and the way it was before.

It is the morning of my birthday.

PART VI

2012

Chapter 30 ~ February

Tad reappeared this weekend. In an email, he mentioned that he would probably be back in the state, but carefully explained, multiple times, that no time was reserved to spend with me. His excuses insulted me. An honest explanation might have helped, but he supplied ridiculous justifications instead: his rental car mileage might be restricted; he had to work every hour of the day and wouldn't be allowed to come home at all. He could not disguise his intent. His words were so outrageous that they could only be lies. They were difficult to read. He used to make excuses and do anything to see me. Now he's doing the same not to.

Every phone conversation or email has been troublesome lately. I can't decide what's worse, waiting for a communication that doesn't come or having one that leaves me disappointed.

Whatever I feel, something between us has changed, no matter how many times he tells me otherwise. With every conversation now, I become more conscious of how young he is. He aspires to be cold and calculating, but most of the time his hurt and anger are apparent. He doesn't yet comprehend that quitting is taking the easy way out. He perceives it as a sign of strength when he separates himself and walks away.

My emails and conversations must have angered or upset him. I asked pointed questions about what happened between us but his vague answers only clouded the issue. I attempted to have a conversation about how his abrupt change in behavior disappointed me, but it revolved only around the emotions I expressed. His remained concealed. That Tuesday was always the elephant in the room.

His communications transformed into details about other girls he's pursuing and the complexities of their relationships. He reveals these interactions with other women, but refuses to discuss what happened between us openly and honestly.

I've glimpsed him through the window a few times over the weekend, but I make a conscious effort not to look. His excuses proved unfounded. He didn't inform me he was coming or bother to call. The disregard hurts more than authentic discussion ever could.

As I approach disintegration with Tad, my relationship with Ethan steadily improves, which is ironic. On some level, perhaps he acknowledges how perilously close to the edge of our marriage I strayed, or maybe the transformation within me intrigues him. Sleep still eludes me. I discarded the underwear from that day with Tad, but I still can't approach half of the clothes in my closet because they invoke memories of him.

Somehow, this entire mess has gone full circle. In the beginning, Ethan reduced me to a shell and Tad provided an escape, an impulse to conceal the pain. But during that, I transferred something to Tad that never should have been his. Not my body, although that never should have been his, either, but I relinquished that part of myself that trusts no one. I haven't showed anyone that side of me since I revealed it to Ethan over fourteen years ago. And the harsh truth is that Tad never earned it. A few weeks of flirting shouldn't have been enough for me to surrender as freely and completely as I did. But my marriage, that began with a passion and a determination to face the world together, became a routine of taking out the garbage, Ethan pestering me to have sex, and sitting in the exact same spot on the sofa in front of the TV every night. The impulsiveness and passion fell away, and we were left with only a lot of things we'd spent our lives working for because we thought we wanted them. The sad fact is that I was lonely.

So now I tremble every time I slink to my garage because I cannot predict how I might react if I bump into Tad. Ethan buttresses me, holding me up. Consistency comforts me. It is easier to stifle my thoughts as I listen to Ethan and Maya review spelling words at the dining room table while I cook dinner. Tad barges, uninvited, into my mind a thousand times a day, but Ethan distracts me with a kiss or a conversation about work and makes it easier to forget.

Internally, I recognize that the time has come to release Tad, but I can't accept it. On Sunday morning, it occurs to me that he will return to his class that afternoon, and if I want to see him in person, I will have to initiate it because he won't. My mind resists, yearning for the strength to construct a wall, force him out, and hurt him in the same way he has punctured me. But I don't. Something within me longs for him to comprehend the damage he has created.

Ethan goes out to grab some donuts, and, while he is gone, I fire off a quick text. "Sorry about everything. I didn't mean for it to turn into this mess."

Tad responds quickly, "Do you want to talk?"

"Maybe around noon. Let me figure out how to escape from the house and I'll let you know."

I distract myself for the rest of the morning, reviewing pronouns with Zach and helping Maya gather supplies to make a poster describing how Tennessee became a state. The entire time, my mind spins round and round devising a plan to circumvent Ethan. On the weekends Ethan now remains in town instead of traveling to athletic events; there is an expectation that we are inseparable. Finally, I default to my standard escape: the gym. I text Tad and tell him to meet me in the parking lot at noon.

Leaving my house, I kiss Ethan goodbye. He hugs me and, instead of releasing, holds on tight. As I pull away, he restrains me and looks directly into my eyes. "You know I love you, right?"

"Yes."

He stares at me intently, scrutinizing. I recognize a fire in his eyes that I haven't seen for years. Ethan is evaluating me, wanting me to choose to remain here with him. I can feel it. He is searching, trying to unearth his connection with me.

"I—" I start to offer to stay, bypass the gym for the day, and resist Tad, but I stutter and stop. "Do you want me to stay home?" I finally ask.

"No," he says and the moment passes. "Have a good workout. Then come home and show me a good time," Ethan flirts, then disappears to break up a Lego fight in the basement.

At the gym, I park near the back of the lot and remain in my car, gazing out over the pool where I've watched my children learn to swim. Before Tad arrives, I try to decide on a neutral opening to our conversation. Given the choice, I would prefer this not be adversarial, but I will be surprised if it isn't. When he knocks on the car window, I startle.

"Hop in," I say, and motion to the passenger seat.

Tad strides around the car and climbs in. His demeanor belies any connection between us. He offers no smile, no greeting kiss, and no eye contact. He perches in the seat, sunglasses on, and faces directly forward, sulking.

"So," I say, "I guess I'll start. Yes, I'm upset. No, I don't fixate on this every minute of every day or obsess about it all the time, but yes, it bothers me. It bothers me that you didn't call after our morning together when you knew how I struggled with the decision to go through with it. It bothers me that all of our communication since that day has been impersonal. It bothers me that you persist in telling me that nothing has changed when it obviously has. Either you're intentionally lying to me or you're lying to yourself. You know I care about you. I told you that I was starting to fall in love with you before you moved, and well before you slept with me. I told you that it was body and soul together or nothing at all. And you encouraged it. But now you keep implying that I should somehow magically know that everything's fine between us. But it *isn't* fine. It has changed. You don't contact me; I initiate our conversations and, when I do, you devise excuses to avoid it. We both know that you make time for what's important to you. So I want to understand what happened. I want to know what changed. Did being together just not hold the same importance for you that it did for me? Did I completely misread all of this?"

Tad shoots me a defensive look, then glares back at the pool. "I've been busy. I know you're a stay-at-home parent, but I'm busy building my career and my life. It isn't easy. I finally received a paycheck after waiting a month, and it won't come close to covering the bills I racked up. They sent me back to take this class and if I don't pass, I lose my job. I can't get along with the group of people they've assigned me to work with. I'm not like everyone else. Things don't just magically happen for me. Half the time, they don't happen even if I work for them. So I'm working my ass off, hoping it'll be enough. I called a few people on the way into town to try to make plans, and not one of them called me back. Everything's exactly the same." He halts and takes a deep breath, then adds, "I thought you were different, but it turns out you're just the same as everyone else."

I freeze, then gasp as I realize I'm literally holding my breath. Exactly the same? The last time he was here, he called me first to announce that he was coming home. The last time he was here, he couldn't control himself, even when Ethan was home. The last time he was here, he pulled me to my basement, petitioning me for sex. The last time he was here, he certainly didn't imply that I was similar to anyone else when he made love to me.

"Tad. Stop and focus. Would you please take off your sunglasses and look at me?" The pause gives me time to check my anger in a manner similar to that required when I discipline my children. Not only does he obviously not appreciate what I risked to have sex with him, but apparently even the act itself wasn't worth the bother because now I'm the same as everyone else.

Annoyed, he pushes the sunglasses back on his head. His eyes are hard and cruel; I almost wish he had refused and left the glasses on. But I need to see them. I need to know if what I say strikes home.

"Do you realize what you just said? First, you haven't addressed anything between us. You and me," I make it clear. "Not everyone else. Not what is happening out there. What is happening *here*. Do you realize that you're complaining to me about people not responding to you? Did it ever cross your mind that someone was waiting, wanting to hear from you, and you didn't even bother to call? That you're so busy chasing people who don't care that you completely ignored the one who was willing to give up everything for you? How does that make me just like everyone else?"

"People just use me," he says. "They're my friends when they need something. In school, people would be nice to me just to persuade me to help with their projects. It is never simply because they want to know me."

Good Lord. He doesn't understand me at all. He is so lost in himself, lost in the way other people have treated him, that he doesn't comprehend the offering I have placed at his feet. He either doesn't realize or doesn't appreciate that the only thing I want from him is him. I don't want him to lose himself in me. I just want to be a part of his life, although I'm starting to wonder why. I'm reasonably certain he isn't the one who was used in this situation.

"I'm not the kind of guy to call and tell you what happened to me during the day. I don't want to talk about what I had for lunch or who did what at work. When I talk, it means I have something to say. I talk to you more than anyone else, including my parents. I work sometimes up to twelve hours a day. I barely sleep six hours at night. There's no time to relax or do anything I want to do. And you're not going to be my top priority. You might make it into the top five, but no person will ever be above my job, myself, and the things I need to do. And I do need to have other relationships outside of this one."

"I understand that." I take a deep breath. "But I thought we agreed on all of this in advance. If not, what was all that talking for? You knew this was emotional for me, not physical. I thought this bond was something that we shared, something that existed outside the boundaries of our normal lives, something special and private. It isn't the amount of time we spend talking that bothers me as much as the content. You dropped this relationship in the realm of laundry and dishes. It's a chore. There's no emotion. You compare your contact with me to checking in with your parents, which I know you only do out of obligation. And if this isn't emotional for me, it isn't anything, because I have plenty of friends. And I don't fuck any of them. I don't expect you to interrupt your life for me, but that's because I presumed I wasn't an interruption. I assumed that I was a part of your life, the same way I accepted you into mine, not just a casual observer. I thought we were closer than that."

"I can't do it," Tad says. "I'm not capable of that kind of relationship."

That is a blatant lie. We already had that type of relationship. I've seen it in him and I've felt it from him. He tries to justify his fabrication. "Some days I wake up and I wish someone was there, but most days I don't. I like being on my own. I don't want the responsibility of having to answer to someone for every choice I make."

"Tad." I brush his arm and he jumps. "I'm not asking to move in or for you to call every day or text every fifteen minutes. And what choices am I asking you to answer for? All I want is for us to return to that place where we've already been. We were close, and then you abruptly disappeared. It hurts and confuses me because you say one thing but then your actions oppose your words. You claim nothing has changed, but it has. Now our conversations revolve around other girls and your interest in them. You didn't do that before we had sex. I'm not an insecure person, but I'm very timid about this because every time I start to trust you, you contradict yourself and force me to reevaluate everything."

"Okay," he says, "then I won't. There, I said it. All right?" Tad is angry now. "I won't. I won't open up anymore. This is as far as it goes. We can either be friends or we can walk away right now."

I survey him from across the console. He silently glares at me. The tension wraps its way over my soul and climbs my body like a vine. My final chance has arrived, my last opportunity. I see the impending end to this conversation. In one swift motion, my hand slides up the back of Tad's neck, grasping him to me, and, in my mind, I kiss him goodbye. As my tongue delves into his mouth, probing one last time, he stiffly responds, voiding any prospects for reconciliation. We part with an awkward silence.

"Are you sure?" I inquire, catching his frigid eyes one last time. "Completely sure?"

"Yes," he states with finality. "Stella, I want to be your friend. I think you're smart and I enjoy talking to you, but it can't go any further than that now. If you want, we can try to stay in touch more, but it will just be as friends."

I already know my answer. The truth is, I've avoided it for a while now, because it means I have to deal with my indiscretion—and my loneliness—on my own. It forces me to acknowledge the fact that I risked my marriage for a man who never loved me and never even professed to. It requires me to admit that I gave much more than I received, and it left a gaping hole that no one can fill but me.

I can't be his friend. I want to be. I want to be so much more than that. But if I agree to friendship, I will check my email every day and wonder why he doesn't write. I will check my phone and wonder if he will text. I will stay perpetually in a state of revolving around him that won't do either one of us any good. And I can't be a good friend to him. A good friend gives impartial advice. A good friend isn't jealous and doesn't make decisions based on how someone's actions affect them personally. I can't detach myself enough emotionally to not feel jealous or want more right now.

Besides, he can't wiggle off the hook like that. Being able to say, "We're still friends," is the easy out for him. It means he doesn't have to admit that he essentially used me and dumped me. He won't be the bad guy because we'd still be friends. I won't let him off that easy.

I can't continue ignoring my own life. Tad never asked for that and never wanted it from me. The truth is that I never meant to give it. But I don't have a magic on/off switch to flip from one mode to another. This relationship between us was a slow build and the dismantling of it may take nearly as long. If only I had realized sooner the damage it would cause. On the outside, both of our lives are unchanged and everything will continue without interruption, but on the inside I grapple to resolve my conflicting emotions.

"Disappear," is the only word that escapes.

He looks at me, disbelief plainly written on his face. That was probably the last answer he expected, but it's my only remaining option. I want to plead with him to stay. I want him to convince me that we will span this divide. I want him to at least care enough to try to convince me that, even as we separate, he cares about me. But I understand him enough to realize that will never happen.

"It is the only way," I say. Now my eyes focus on the pool as my surroundings fade and acceptance flows through me.

He turns in silence, climbs out, and slams the car door, trapping me in the destiny I chose.

Chapter 31 ~ April

I wake with my heart racing and curl against Ethan's chest to contain my panic. Everything inside me is broken. My ears listen to the silence, searching for demons that reside in unfamiliar noises instead of whirling through my mind.

Tad was in town this past weekend. I knew he'd returned when a rental car appeared in the driveway, but he avoided me and I didn't contact him, even though I started to a hundred times. I spent the entire weekend distracting myself with every maintenance project I could find. When I finally saw him, I'd just walked out of a hardware store with some Endust and a hinge to repair our fireplace door. As I buckled my seatbelt and looked in my mirror, I saw him approaching the door to the same store with his brother. He stopped and met my eyes in the mirror, holding them long enough for our entire final conversation to flash through my head. The words, "You're just like everyone else," prevented me from reacting or even acknowledging him. I fled as if I didn't recognize him. I think those are the most awful words anyone has ever spoken to me. Of all the things Tad is or isn't, he will never be just like anyone else to me.

As I snuggle into Ethan, he rolls toward me and wraps me in his arms. His nose nuzzles into my hair. "Bad dream?"

"Yeah," I answer. Memories of Tad flood my mind. I love him. It's distinct from the way I feel about anyone else. He isn't the center of my life, he isn't Ethan, but he is still important to me.

"Tell me about it. You'll feel better." Ethan is asking me to confide in him and I don't know where to even begin. My sobs calm to just tears racing down my face. I should feel guilt, yet I don't. I feel fear. I fear that he'll discover this indiscretion and that it will break our family apart. I fear that I'll be forced to find a job and relegate my children to childcare. But not guilt. I didn't cheat Ethan out of anything. He let it go.

I search frantically to design my lie. "I dreamed I was riding in an elevator. As it rose, I huddled in the corner with my hands over my ears, screaming."

"What were you screaming about, Stella?"

"I don't remember." I never thought I was capable of such hypocrisy, and especially not of sustaining such a huge deception without ever feeling remorse.

"Everything is okay," Ethan comforts me.

Everything is not okay. I am a wreck. The sky is still dark, but I roll to my side of the bed. "I think I'll go for a run. It will help me shut my brain off."

"I'm going back to sleep." Ethan yawns as he twists under the covers. "Come find me when you're finished."

I peck him lightly on the cheek and dress quickly. As I creep down the steps, I pass the fan in the kids' bathroom. Tad was a part of my life for so long that even insignificant things maintain an association with him. His parents' house and his empty parking spot loom next door as I flee from them. He invades the space surrounding me.

My pace automatically kicks in, but the blare from my iPod headphones can't block out the emotions compressed inside me. They ricochet around, searching for an outlet, spinning me in circles and dropping me back in the same place I began: confused and alone.

Anger erupts and my pace quickens. How could he? How could he destroy our emotional, magical, separate connection and black out those few hours we spent together? I can't forgive him. He didn't call. We didn't discuss what happened or how we felt about it. He took something special and smothered it into the one thing I feared the most: nothing.

One. Two. One. Two. My feet pound the ground. It takes two. He was just as active a participant as I was. During our initial conversation, I was searching for confirmation that our relationship was not a figment of my imagination. The only thing I hoped would result from it was that he and I would stay in contact as friends. I expected some harmless flirting, but nothing more. When the physical came into play, he was just as interested in avoiding reality as I was and he desired it just as much as I did. I never removed my wedding ring. I picked up the phone when Ethan called. I never pretended to be anything but married, even if that marriage wasn't meeting my needs. And I was very open and honest that my connection with Tad was emotional, not just physical.

When we crossed that physical line, the emotion that came with it was more than I ever bargained for. I thought I could separate it, this tiny little secret escape from reality that was just for him and me. And at first that was what it was and I had exactly what I wanted. I thought I was a part of his life and I made him a part of mine. The truth is that he never did know all of me. He just found the one portion of me that no one else could reach.

My rhythm steadies as my anger subsides. On rational days, on the days I believe that I can return to my ordinary life sometime in the future, I can almost distinguish Tad from the idea I embellished him to be. I appreciate that he's young. He has no real life experiences to guide him. Heck, he'd never even held a job. He's overwhelmed with becoming an adult and taking responsibility for his own life. He's scared and he's lonely. I admit that I encouraged him into an awkward, no win situation. He doesn't have any relationships that he can depend on to support him. If he exposes too much of himself to me, it's with the full understanding that I belong to someone else, and, even if I didn't, we'd be in two completely different stages of our lives and a real relationship would be highly improbable, if not impossible.

The tree that marks my two mile accomplishment flies past and I turn the corner to aim myself home. I feel like two people crammed into the same body. Some days, I love who I am and what Ethan and I have accomplished. I look around our neighborhood and realize that we almost have nothing to want. We have been so fortunate. I think of Maya and Zach, tucked under their covers at home, and I realize how lucky we are to have children who are for the most part healthy, intelligent, happy little people. But the other person in me screams to break free. She feels trapped under the weight of the responsibility of life. She loves Ethan, but also knows that the passion and connection in the relationship have broken due to the strain of reality. And she looked to Tad to escape that reality and to have a connection with a man who understood that one part that Ethan couldn't for a while. I did. I looked to Tad to escape my life and to test my relationship with Ethan. Was it over with him? Now I know it wasn't, but at the time I really believed it was. I review our useless fights over and over in my mind. The weeks of not speaking to each other and of shutting each other out to the point that I felt that anyone, even this young boy who truly couldn't understand the complexities of my life, could understand me better than my own husband.

I'm running the last leg to home. The song Tad sang on the way to the airport cycles up on my iPod and knocks down the walls I spent the past twenty-eight minutes constructing. By allowing everything with him to become so skewed and blown out of proportion, I have lost him completely. Desperation overwhelms me, pushing me to contact him. I could stop right now, in the middle of the street, and text or call him. That thought itself tells me I shouldn't. If I feel that type of need, of yearning, then I'm not approaching him out of friendship, but out of again wanting something from him that he's already clearly stated he will not give. I cannot invite him back into my life until I can find a point where I can maintain a neutral friendship, and that will mean respecting his wishes if he doesn't want to be mine. Anything other than that will annihilate me and won't be fair to him.

How weak am I? He didn't even call after he fucked me. I should be able to get through a run without him.

I see no way out. I drown day by day and minute by minute in a pool of my own making. The uncertainty makes it worse, because I understand that I deserve it. I convince myself that if I can absorb all the pain, capture it inside, and punish myself enough then maybe Ethan and my family will be spared. I know it's illogical, but I will suffer all of it if it means I can protect him, protect all of them, so that my family doesn't fall apart.

My family. My home. I turn onto my street. *Mine.* Once or twice, I've felt flashes of forgiving both him and myself, but they fade as quickly as they appear. I don't think I'll ever achieve either. As I turn into my driveway, my gaze oscillates between my front door and the empty space where Tad's car used to reside.

The morning rushes by. Once the kids are at school, I hide in the house in the dark, dressed to go to the gym, crying. Tad did what I asked him to do. He disappeared. Not one email, not one phone call, not one text. He even un-friended me online.

I open the computer to pay the bills, but I reread the emails Tad sent me instead. I saved them all. As I read, the disappointment pushes through my chest all over again. He took my escape from reality and threw it into the mud of the mundane. I realized that I will probably never feel that way again, so I pushed harder, and then he arrogantly demoted me to his friend. I already know what he thinks of his friends and for him to say that is derogatory. The insult doesn't resonate without knowing him personally. He doesn't trust or even particularly like most of his friends.

He didn't crush me. The weight of my life did, along with the realization that there is nothing left to look forward to. I've been to Oz and seen the wizard. I know that nothing is magical, that every beautiful moment has its price. And so I guess this continuous pain and losing him is the price I pay for this experience. I don't know if it was worth it or not. I love that I lived my fantasy, but if I lost his friendship entirely in exchange for that little bit of time, I will regret it forever. Not the act itself, but the fact that it pushed him away from me instead of sealing the connection that I naively hoped could sustain us both.

The truth is that if there were no lasting impacts, no children's lives to destroy, and no huge age difference, I would love a chance to have a real relationship with Tad. But he told me in no uncertain terms that he doesn't want that. And, in reality, it never was an option. Ethan and I have spent years destroying each other. The only real options available to me are either to try to work out some type of understanding with Ethan or to leave him and move on alone.

It is time to begin the rest of my story now. What happened with Tad happened. It is sad and I hate the way it ended, but it is over. The question is, where do I go from here? Where do I want to go? If I could be anywhere, anyone, a year from now, what would I choose?"

I close my eyes and inhale. It is time. One by one, I delete each message, tears streaming down my face as I confirm that, yes, I do want to delete them permanently. When the final one disappears, I cancel the entire account. Gone, as if it never existed.

***

Ethan is sitting at the computer when I walk in the door from dropping Zach off at soccer practice. He looks over and asks, "What's going on at Maya's school? I saw on the caller ID that they called again."

"Don't ask," I snap.

"Did something happen?" He glances back at the monitor, reading the sports. I do not want to have this discussion with him because I already know where it is headed. In his mind, it'll be my fault, whatever it is.

"Trust me, you don't want to hear it. Just stay out of it."

"But I'm asking you," he challenges me as he meets my eyes.

"I said something I shouldn't have. I was venting about homework to another parent, who also happens to teach at the school. Since she thought my points were valid, she suggested to the principal that we discuss it. Now they're trying to drag me into meetings to critique the teachers. The last thing I want to do is sit in a meeting so they can justify watching movies in class and then assigning two hours worth of homework.

"Go ahead, say it. It's my own fault. That it's what I deserve for opening my mouth in this fucking town. But I'm not you. I can't live like a robot and talk to no one. So I'm sorry, I was blowing off steam and, believe me, I'm being punished for it. I don't need you to rub it in."

Ethan is frustrated—I can tell by the look on his face—but instead of stomping off, he shuts down the computer browser, walks over to me, and pulls my hip bones towards his, nipping at my lip.

"Stop it," I yell and push him back. My emotions graze the surface today; I can't drown them. "Why do you think you have the right to maul me every time I'm pissed at you?"

"Stella, I'm trying to comfort you," Hurt seeps into Ethan's voice.

"Comfort me? You don't comfort me by grinding against me," I spew. "I can't remember the last time you comforted me. There is no one I can talk to. I live in a cage. I talk to no one. No one comforts me or wants my opinion. So why am I expected to ram my tongue down your throat in appreciation?"

"Stella, I'm trying to comfort you in the only way I know how." Ethan slumps against me. But he didn't pick up a vacuum to tune me out.

I wait in silence, inviting him to continue. My patience is rewarded.

"When I reach for you, how do you not comprehend that it's because I miss you? I don't know how to make you understand. When you're upset, your emotions kick into overdrive. I can't process information the way you do. It doesn't mean I don't care. It means this is the only way I know to show you. And you hate me for it. You evaluate everything. You have an opinion on everything. You analyze politics and religion and the cell phone bill. I'm simple. I want to enjoy my life, to eat, sleep, exercise, and make love to you. I can't give you what you need intellectually. I never could. I know that. The kids come at us from all angles. We have almost no time together, and the time we have is disjointed, squeezed between the hours a babysitter is available and not when we actually want or need to be together. I prioritize myself because I have to stay strong. Strong enough to take care of myself, strong enough to love you even though we both feel alone. So I'm sorry. I'm sorry I pulled you to me. But it's my way of telling you that I do want to hear it. You shut me out."

His insight defuses my anger. He is right. I have been angry at Ethan for years because he has not met my needs, wants, or expectations. I punished him by pulling away from him.

I balance on the brink of a revelation that might alter my entire life.

All these years, in my mind, Ethan continually disappointed me. But when I review my list of grievances, they wither under the scrutiny; some of them date back years. Yes, we have some serious problems, but none are insurmountable. He is faithful to me. He loves me and provides for me. He gives me complete freedom to create my own destiny and allocates space for me to grow.

I am the one who locks him out. I created the chasm in our relationship by setting the expectation that he could fill my emptiness. When he couldn't, and when I finally accepted he never would, Tad slid into that space and for a moment I didn't feel so alone.

I want the connection I felt with Tad, but to Ethan. I want him to come to me with passion, not an obligatory bedtime send-off. I want him to desire me emotionally, not just physically, to show interest in my day, my opinions, my successes, and my failures. I want for him to prioritize *us*, to anticipate spending time with me. I want us to build an impenetrable bond that restores our relationship to a point where I can honestly call him my best friend. I want to sever this connection in my soul to Tad so that we can return to a more appropriate friendship. I would like to know the other sides of him without all of this tension between us. I would like to be the friend to him that I originally intended to be before the rest of this interfered.

"You are right." Foreign words erupt from my mouth. Ethan peers at me in disbelief. "I expect the worst from you at all times because that is the way I perceive it. I never consider it from your point of view."

Ethan's hand entwines with mine. He sits on the sofa and pulls me close next to him, but not on top of him. Not with expectation. And he talks to me.

Whack. Whack. My arms smack the water as they pinwheel and I glide through my lane.

For the past three months, I've spent an enormous amount of time focusing on myself. I started by registering for another mini-triathlon, similar to the one Alyssa and I did years ago together. Swimming every day gave me a goal to work for, and concentrating so much energy on my physical movements was a fantastic way to shut my mind off. Some days I trained so hard that I vomited. Those days, I reminded myself to surrender while the emotions washed through me; the exercise shouldn't be self punishment.

I decided to stay in Nashville for the entire weekend of the competition instead of just one night. Ethan didn't criticize me; actually, he encouraged it. I felt selfish for allocating the money to spend time alone, but burned myself a new CD for the car and sang at the top of my lungs with the windows down.

Focus. The rhythm of my breathing synchronizes with my arms automatically. I flip turn and ease past the guy sharing my lane.

He introduced himself before the race began. Theo. An uncomfortable coincidence. "So have you done one of these before?" he asked, trying to fill the silence as we finished our paperwork and claimed our goodie bags. Theo's eyes wandered down my body and my mind jumped to Tad immediately. His memory still pops in to visit at random unexpected times.

"A few years ago," I dismissed him vaguely.

"Do you work around here?" This guy didn't take a hint.

"Nope. I'm a stay-at-home mom. My husband is keeping our kids so I can enjoy a weekend on my own."

That shut him up.

As I pull ahead, I am conscious of my kick. What do my legs look like under the water? Is my suit in place over my ass? Distracted, I inhale water and miss my next breath, destroying my rhythm. I gasp and slow to a breast stroke to clear my airway.

Theo sails past. I have lost my momentum because of another man. I run from Tad. I dance around Ethan. Now I choke for Theo. Where am I in this? I define myself in relation to a man. Apparently any man. Even an unfamiliar one swimming next to me. The more I consider it, the more I realize that I always have. Perhaps this is the hurdle, not the challenge of finding what I want in any of them, but the courage to provide what I need for myself.

I suck in a giant breath and drive myself after him. My goggles steam up and I can't see the end of the pool, but it doesn't matter. My muscles scream. I'm not sure I know myself at all. But I'm going to. It is time to love myself with no expectation.

***

Through the bicycling and running portions of the competition, I block out my surroundings, focus only on myself, and work. By the time I complete the course, I don't even care how I finish or score. It is nice to complete it and list it as an accomplishment, but achieving my goal and gratifying myself is the important part.

***

Jonathan, the guy I used to work for, and I sit at dinner. My arms ache, reminding me of the race this morning every time I pick up my fork. He was my boss, but also my best friend for a long time. When I quit, I pulled back from the friendship because it would have been too hard to move on otherwise. But being together again, our conversation picks up as if we spoke yesterday, even though it's been years.

"You wouldn't believe the people we've hired and fired since you left. I've supervised five engineers. Five. You've only been gone seven years. Not one of them is competent," he complains. "You aren't willing to move back are you? I can assemble a relocation package by Monday."

"I wish," I reply. A sliver of me would love that, but right now Maya and Zach are happy and stable. Ethan is steadily moving up through hospital management. We're not in a place where we are ready to leave.

"Me, too. A project landed on my desk that would be perfect for you. I travel at least three weeks a month now that I'm with corporate. I can't manage it myself and no one else on staff has the knowledge to even attempt it. Want it?"

"You're joking, right?" I smile. "I'd love it. I haven't worked in seven years. Hell, I'll do it for free if you'll pay my babysitter and get me out of the house."

"We can pay you more than that," he says seriously. He bends down to his briefcase leaning against the chair under the table, pulls out a packet that was obviously prepared for this moment, and tosses it in front of me. "Take it home and read it. If you're interested, send me a detailed estimate and we'll set you up as a vendor. You can invoice us by the month. And you can write most of the manuals from home. Then you can travel to the lab for a few days, implement your work, and we can have lunch."

It's the perfect job for me. I already know almost all of the employees, a lot of their strengths and weaknesses, and who I can call for what information to work efficiently. "I'll consider it." The only thing that stalls my acceptance is Ethan's reaction.

While driving from the restaurant to my hotel, I dial Ethan. "Hey, you'll never guess what happened." I eagerly open the conversation.

"You landed a job?" Ethan predicts my announcement correctly, agitating me.

"Thanks a lot. Way to make it not seem so exciting."

"So tell me about it," he encourages.

The details tumble over each other to spill out, trying to convince him of their validity.

"Stella, it sounds perfect for you," he agrees. "We'll have to come up with a plan to juggle the kids for the days you won't be home. Maybe I'll ask my sister if she'd be willing to nanny part time. I'll just schedule vacation on the days she isn't available."

I had assumed this conversation would upset him. I never imagined that he would enthusiastically help me arrange a schedule.

My confidence swells. I can do this. I accept that this phase of my life, staying home and giving up everything for my family, is coming to an end. This is the progression I am meant to follow. It's time.

***

Settled into my hotel, I lie flat on the bed, staring at the ceiling. Months ago I would have given anything for this time alone. I would have texted Tad immediately and wanted to talk all night. But the silence beckons; my thoughts revel in the freedom to whirl through my mind.

From this distance, I can see that my anger and hurt towards Tad sprang from his lack of acknowledgement or appreciation. His need to separate himself from the emotion panicked me as I searched for reassurance. And I pushed too hard, presumed too much at a time when he needed support and had little to give. I pursued him so frantically that I looked past him. I floundered to retain the feeling of being understood, of being accepted, of being loved. When I expected nothing, Tad gave all. But when my expectations overwhelmed him, he fled.

He *did* stay in contact after our morning together, even while juggling his new life. But the lag time before the phone call undermined my trust. I interpreted it as rejection. His silence insulted me; it was a slap in the face. My insecurity and anger overshadowed every other emotion.

Even at the end, he offered to communicate more often. But I didn't believe him.

I may never be able to sever the connection I feel to Tad, but I will spend the rest of my life trying to, and hopefully at some point it won't have to be such a conscious effort. It doesn't mean that what I feel isn't still there. Isn't there some quote about how a mind, once expanded, never returns to its original dimensions? Perhaps I can never go back to my original dimensions, but I can continue to grow. Either way, I have to let him go. Completely. But I am content; the confirmation that our bond wasn't a product of my imagination is enough.

I open my phone and scroll down the contacts. Tad's number glares at me from the screen. Another opportunity. I might call and he might be thrilled to hear from me. But I won't. I delete the contact, allowing the final tether between us to snap.

As I plug the charger into the base of the phone, my background, a picture of Ethan, flashes. Extricating Tad from my mind has been difficult, even though I haven't seen or spoken to him again. Every time I find myself thinking about him, I focus that energy on Ethan. If I miss Tad's flirty texts, I send Ethan a text at work. When I think about the things I wanted to explore with Tad, the things I fantasized about, I surprise Ethan with them instead.

Ethan has responded to the attention in ways I never expected. He listens to me again. I feel like he sees me. Not all the time, not every day. There are still outside pressures, kids pushing us apart, bills to pay, and those lousy days when one or the other of us wants to hide under a rock. But he asks how my day was and he kisses me, really kisses me, not just a perfunctory peck. He kisses me good morning. He kisses me on the way out the door to work. He kisses me when he walks through the door most evenings. He also stays home a lot more, but not because I request it. Last weekend, he actually turned down a poker night. I didn't ask him to and didn't even know he did it until afterward, but we had been in sync all afternoon. Later that evening, he said that we connect so rarely that we have to stop and appreciate it when we can. There is a thin floss of hope with him that flickers occasionally, I think we both realize how fragile we are right now.

My relationship with Ethan can never go back to what it was. We hit my breaking point and I broke. And I'm glad I did, because it provided an opportunity to build something different, something better for myself. Ironically, I think everything I've experienced might give me a chance to save my marriage. If we can find each other and reconnect, that will be wonderful, but our relationship will never revert to our previous state because I won't allow it. I won't trap myself in that situation again. So if we can't find each other, I will accept that as well. I see no where to go but up, regardless of whether he is by my side or not.

I walk to the mirror, unzip my polka-dot cosmetics bag, and begin my evening routine. I am tired. Mentally. Physically. Emotionally. The washcloth scratches along my eyelids as my make-up dissolves away. I'm working on myself. I wish I could say that everything is perfect now. I wish I could find a simple solution and happy ending for myself. But I don't really believe in happy endings. I'm an engineer. Absolute zero can only be approached, never achieved, so the best I hope for is continuous improvement. And I achieved that, continuous improvement, I mean. I am happier than I've been in a long time.

My reflection smiles back at me. Pimples. Crow's feet. Grey hairs. They are mine. I smile. I actually smile. I like this feeling. From now on, I plan to save myself.

I have hatched. My shell is gone, but so are the cracks.

About the Author

Stella Maddox earned her Bachelor's in Chemical Engineering from the University of Akron in 1998. She left industry in 2005 to stay home with her children. In addition to writing, she serves as a freelance industrial environmental consultant and balances a husband, three children, and two cats. She and her family reside in southern Ohio.

ALL THINGS THAT MATTER PRESS, INC.

FOR MORE INFORMATION ON TITLES AVAILABLE FROM
ALL THINGS THAT MATTER PRESS, GO TO
http://allthingsthatmatterpress.com
or contact us at
allthingsthatmatterpress@gmail.com